I0660084

LAURA LUKASAVAGE

Moonlight Secrets

Copyright © 2024 by Laura Lukasavage

All rights reserved. No part of this publication may be reproduced, stored or transmitted in any form or by any means, electronic, mechanical, photocopying, recording, scanning, or otherwise without written permission from the publisher. It is illegal to copy this book, post it to a website, or distribute it by any other means without permission.

This novel is entirely a work of fiction. The names, characters and incidents portrayed in it are the work of the author's imagination. Any resemblance to actual persons, living or dead, events or localities is entirely coincidental.

Laura Lukasavage asserts the moral right to be identified as the author of this work.

Laura Lukasavage has no responsibility for the persistence or accuracy of URLs for external or third-party Internet Websites referred to in this publication and does not guarantee that any content on such Websites is, or will remain, accurate or appropriate.

Designations used by companies to distinguish their products are often claimed as trademarks. All brand names and product names used in this book and on its cover are trade names, service marks, trademarks and registered trademarks of their respective owners. The publishers and the book are not associated with any product or vendor mentioned in this book. None of the companies referenced within the book have endorsed the book.

First edition

ISBN: 978-1-956994-09-4

Editing by Josie O'Brien
Cover art by Laura Lukasavage

This book was professionally typeset on Reedsy.
Find out more at reedsy.com

To the best man I've ever known. Who showed me how a man should treat and love a woman. A hard worker, a jack of all trades, strong, loving, and caring, would give the shirt off his back. They don't make them like him anymore. My gpop, papi to my children. I'm blessed to have had him and so glad my children do. I hope you all have a papi like him.

Contents

Acknowledgement

I would also like to thank Josie O'Brien and Marlena Guzowski for their dedication and free help and time in editing to make this book the best it can be. I would be lost without them and all the others who have helped along the way.

Also, a special thanks to all my loyal followers and you, my readers, for without you this would all be pointless.

Prologue

Some time ago:

Jocelyn

As I move deeper into the depths of the dark forest surrounding my home, a strong feeling of unease fills my stomach. My nervousness triggers beads of sweat to form on my skin, running along the length of my collar and down my spine, provoking the little hairs on the back of my neck to stick up as my temperature rises. I turn in every direction, staring into the dark forest to make sure no one is following me, tension spreads through my body, making every muscle tighten. My heart pounds away feverishly inside my warm chest as I take in my surroundings, seeing only trees in all directions. There are no other signs of life.

The forest is soundless.

I move slowly, listening to the stillness in the darkness around me, I must be sure that I am truly alone.

I must not be followed.

Only one thought, one person, continues to run through my mind and that's Aaron.

Even though it's only been a few days since I last saw him, it feels like months. We sneak away from our homes and meet in the depths of the forest at least once a week. Living like this hasn't been easy and we both wish we didn't have to hide our love from our families and the fact that we've known each other for many years but if our families ever knew the truth it would lead to war between our villages. That hatred is something we never want to tarnish our love, so instead we choose to live our lives together in secret knowing that two people cannot change the years of hatred between our worlds. A dislike that started so long ago that no one can be certain of its true origin.

I fear if my parents ever found out about Aaron what the consequences would be for both of us. I wish I could leave with him and never come back but my family would never stop searching for me. Not just because I'm their only child but I'm the next in line to rule our village. It has always been our bloodline who has led our kind and there is no changing what is expected of me. If I was ever to take off with Aaron it would only be a matter of time before they found me and then what? I know and the outcome is too horrible to think about.

I've seen this world change in so many ways over my years, but one thing that hasn't changed, and probably never will, is the hatred between our villages. I, myself, don't understand what could have taken place so many years ago to have created this divide.

A sound echoes from behind me, triggering my heart to thump wildly in my chest. Panic engulfs my senses, sending my head spinning. I turn around to face the direction in which I heard the noise emerge from, as strong hands embrace my waist and draw me close. A moment later I feel his familiar lips on mine and my body relaxes.

It's *my* Aaron.

He holds me close for a long time, just like me he's not wanting to end our long awaited embrace. After a few minutes he pulls back, locking his eyes with mine.

"I've missed you," He says and kisses me once more.

When our kiss softens I lean away gazing up at him. It had felt like forever since we last saw one another but looking at him now I feel it truly has been a length of time since our last moment together. His once ear length raven hair is now to his shoulder blades, the longest I've ever seen him wear. I try to think about our last meeting but I can't remember how long ago it really was.

"What is it?" Aaron asks.

I smile. "I was just wondering," I pause, not sure how to continue, "How long has it been since our last meeting?"

Aaron's expression changes quickly from joy to uncertainty but I barely have time to notice before he is turning away, "I've been here every night waiting for you, but you never came. At one point I almost walked into your village to find you. "

He must have seen the look of horror on my face because he pauses for a brief moment to lock eyes and then he continues while gesturing to himself, "As you can see I did not."

I think about only three nights ago, when I am sure I saw him last. "How long, Aaron?"

He whispers, "Two months."

My heart skips.

Two months? There's no way. I was just here with him. My thoughts begin to run rampant in my head until Aaron's touch pulls me from them. He presses his hand lightly against my abdomen.

I stare up at him. "What?"

"I'm not sure…I thought I heard something."

Grinning at him my eyes widened. "So you decided to touch my stomach?"

The left side of his mouth rises to meet his cheek. "The noise I heard came from you and you smell…different."

"Ok…So again, you're touching my stomach why?"

Aaron peers from me to his hand that rests on my stomach, "I don't know my hand just went there."

"Of all the places your hand could grab, you go there?" I giggle.

Aaron's smile extends sending the right side of his mouth up to meet the other. "Not now please, I'm being serious."

"When aren't you?" I mumble as I look away.

"Not funny." He grumbles.

I lift my shoulders for a shrug. "I wasn't trying to be."

Aaron removes his hand from my stomach, standing up straight. "What's that supposed to mean?"

"Oh, nothing."

Aaron lifts his right hand and sticks his pointer finger in my face and waves it around playfully. "Don't 'oh nothing' me."

I can't stop the smile from forming on my face. "Or what?"

"I'll show you what."

Aaron lowers his arms and his look is one I know all too well. I turn to run the other way but I'm not fast enough. In seconds he has his arms wrapped around my torso and is turning me back around to face him. The smile on his face is a mask of my own. I wonder how I have survived all my years without him by my side until now.

This time it is me who pulls him in for a kiss. His surprise is evident by how hard his lips are against mine for a moment before we are moving in sync together, his arms moving around my back. He pulls me in as close as possible until our bodies feel like they are melting together.

Aaron moves his hand to my cheek to remove a strand of my hair that escaped the tight bun I put on top of my head only hours before.

"Want to take a walk? Do you have time?" Aaron asks as he takes my small hand in his. The calluses on his palm feel like home as his skin rests against mine.

"Always."

He stops moving forward, "That's not an answer."

"Alright fine," I try to suppress a smile, "My parents were asleep when I left. We should have a few hours and as for the walk that was my answer before."

"Always?"

I nod. "Have a problem with that?"

The smile spreads across his face. "Nope, never."

We walk to the east in the direction of his pack. The night breeze is one I welcome as it passes over my feverish skin. I look around to see the leaves are starting to fall from the trees and land on the rocks below. The night sky is full of stars and as I close my eyes to make a wish Aaron's hand returns to my stomach.

"Not again?" I groan as I open my eyes to leer at him.

His eyes widened before my lips met with his. The kiss is urgent but at the same time he's being weirdly gentle with me. When our kiss ends I ask, "What is it?"

His eyes shine when he replies, "You're pregnant."

Knowing there's no way I heard him correctly, I say, "Can you repeat that, please."

Aaron's smirk grows. "We're going to have a baby."

"What? I think you've finally lost your mind?"

Aaron's grin falters only a little and I have to look to the ground knowing I'm the cause of his happiness dissipating. His free hand comes to rest under my chin making me look back into his eyes that are so full of love and happiness. "No, Jocelyn, you are pregnant."

This has to be a joke. "How?"

His smile returns in full. "Well honey you see when two people come together in a moment of love and passion-"

My eyes go wide as I cut him off, "Don't you dare finish that sentence." I pause, not sure what to say next, "But still it's not possible."

"Well apparently it is. And the smell and noise I heard from you earlier was because I was sensing you were pregnant, but I couldn't get a positive read on it and just now when I touched your stomach again, I saw something."

"What?"

His eyes shone as he removed a piece of hair out of my eyes again, "I wasn't sure if you wanted to know the sex of our child or not?"

Bewildered, I ask, "You know what it is?"

"You're forgetting I have keener hearing and smell and other gifts different from yours. I could hear the second heartbeat coming from you earlier and when I touched your stomach just now, I could see a little girl. Our little girl." Aaron closes his eyes trying to fight back a laugh. "There are many things you still have to learn about what my-kind can do. What I can do."

I smile for the first time at the thought of us becoming parents. I've wanted kids for longer than I can remember and I know Aaron will be a great father so for now the rest of my worries can take a back seat.

Aaron, trying to hold back his excitement, says it one more time, "She's a girl. We are having a daughter."

I smile with him, ear to ear, as he takes my hand and leads me over to a big rock gesturing for me to sit down. Once I'm seated he kneels down next to me placing his hand on my stomach once again, his face becomes one I recognize well and I stifle a laugh. He is trying to concentrate. Moments later he is looking up at me with teary eyes.

"Aaron, what is it, what's wrong is she-"

He cuts me off before the alarm sets in. "She's fine, she's … happy."

Aaron's right, there's still so much I don't understand about his kind and still so much I want to learn. This child is going to be more powerful than we can imagine. Not only will she be the first of her kind but both Aaron and I are the strongest in our villages and that alone would make her stronger than most. But the fact that there has never been anyone like her scares me a little. We know nothing about what powers she could have but if she's anything like her father or me for that matter then that could cause some trouble for us. She will be the first of her kind, a mixed child and many will not like that fact, many will try to hunt us down. I can't help but move my arms around my waist in a protective manner as my mind begins to race. I can't seem to form any words. I've been having dreams about a little girl for a while now and that's another reason why I'm so worried. One of my powers is visions but I only seem to have them when I'm sleeping. Sometimes it's hard to tell the difference between what's the dream and what's the vision. However, now I know all the dreams I've been having about a little girl, my little girl, may come to pass and I fear for her for more reasons than I can count.

What are we going to do? My parents can't find out, they would see her as a danger to our way of living. They won't be able to see her as a way to bring peace between our villages, if peace is even something they want. I've always wondered why my parents seemed so angry whenever I would talk about going outside our village and my dreams only made it clearer to me. They don't care about peace, they like the way we live, they believe in keeping our blood pure as they would say, and our daughter would be considered bad blood to them. When I came into the woods all those years ago, I was doing more than running from my responsibilities, I was running to be free and that's when I met Aaron. He was with some of his pack, they were learning how to shift for the first time. Since that day we became friends and I would sneak out to see him almost every day. We talked and told each other everything and became more than just a safe place for each other but we also became best friends. I wish I could tell my parents what he meant to me and have us all sit around telling stories and laughing with one another, but I know that is a reality I can never have. I made my choice long before tonight. It will always be Aaron.

I know no matter how far I would run they would always find me and when they did, I wouldn't only lose Aaron but now I would also lose my daughter.

The trees begin to move in on me as the night air turns my skin to fire. I try to focus on Aaron's face as it turns black around the edges. My name is the last thing I hear and Aaron's eyes are the last thing I see as I feel my body falling to the hard cold earth.

Chapter 2

Present Day:

Amberly

Being a teenager is tough, there are a million and one things I would love to be able to control or change in my life but as my mother always reminds me I'm not considered an adult till I turn eighteen and even then she's the boss, or so she says.

One thing that would be at the top of my list to change would be carbs. I mean come on I would like to eat how the guys do and not have to worry about my image, then there is the whole standing up to pee thing they got going for them. I mean how convenient is that? But the main thing I would love to change is the ridiculous rule my mother created. The one where my beautiful Triangular Woodlands are off-limits. Our West Virginia lands are full of rocks, trees and hills, our valley is a mix of green and brown. It's my favorite place to be. I feel free and safe when I'm out here like nothing can touch me. My mind is a place that's never quiet, it's always running a mile a minute but out here, it's calm, almost like I'm home. I would give anything to be able to come and go without a worry or in fear that someone will catch me, or I should say us.

Troy and Logan aren't just two guys to me, they are my best friends. I've known them since before I was even born. Yup, you heard that right. See, my mom and their moms grew up together and even though my mom had me a few years later, we were still thrown together like cattle in a pen but as we grew up somewhere along the way, how we became friends seemed to bother us less.

Logan nudges his shoulder into mine, "You OK? You seem quiet today?"

Troy laughs, "Ly, quiet? I think you have the wrong girl there mate. Maybe you're mistaking her for Caterina," he stops to turn around and look back at our home, "but I'm pretty sure we left her back in the village," he turns around to look in my direction, "unless she somehow learned how to possess our little Amberly here without us noticing."

Logan waves him off, "Enough, Troy."

Troy raises his hands in defense, "Hey, I'm just saying don't poke the beast," he lifts his hand to his face and leans in to whisper in Logan's ear, but loud enough for me to still hear, "We can never get her to shut up so let her be, the peace and quiet is wonderful."

I hit him hard on the shoulder.

"Hey, now you know I'm right," Troy says as he runs off.

Logan shakes his head, "Ignore him, he's in a rare mood today."

Despite Troy's annoying as always behavior, there isn't a moment in my life that they haven't been there to share with me and honestly, I wouldn't have it any other way. But if you would have asked any one of us how we felt about each other before the age of ten we would have given you an answer that would show our dislike towards each other.

Logan's voice interrupts my thoughts again, "Amberly?"

"Yeah?"

His grin stops my heart, "You didn't answer me."

I close my eyes trying to think but I don't remember him asking me a question. I open my eyes and return his smile, "Sorry, I don't remember, what did you ask me?"

Logan's voice raises as he laughs, "I asked if you were OK."

"Oh, yeah that question," I let out a little laugh of my own, "Sorry, I'm fine. Just thinking."

"About?"

"The usual."

Logan looks away from me for the first time, "Your mom again?"

Just the mention of her turns my stomach. With my mother being the one in charge of our whole village it makes it a little hard to breathe. Everyone expects so much from me and I always feel like I'm being watched by everyone, so coming out here is like a breath of fresh air that I seem to need regularly. If I knew I could get away with it I would have left home years ago to live in these woods. However, with me being my mother's only child I'm next in line to lead so if I went missing, they would move heaven and earth to find me. Not because I'm her daughter but because I'm the princess, I guess you could call it. See, my mother and I have never been close, and not from the lack of trying on my part either. She's always been so distant and closed off from me and the more I ask her about my father or our family the harder it seems to get. So, I stopped asking her anything and she went one way and I went the other. The only time I see her, or even talk to her for that matter, is when we are training. Whether it be my magic or learning my responsibilities for when I take over. I would be lying if I said it didn't bother me. It's bad enough never knowing my grandparents or my father but in many ways, I could say I don't know my mother either.

"You wanna watch where you're walking." Troy chuckles in my direction.

I look up just in time to see I'm about to walk into a tree. I push down my annoyance towards Troy before it makes its way out to play. He really is a pain in my ass, but I guess that's to be expected. He's more like a brother to me than a friend and even though I don't have any real siblings of my own I've been told that it's normal for them to butt heads now and then, so I guess that's why we get on each other's nerves so much. But Logan is a different story. I guess I haven't looked at him in a brotherly way in years. I know that's how I should see him because we've known each other since we could crawl but somehow, somewhere over the years, it shifted for me. I stopped seeing him as a brother and started seeing him as someone I know will always be there, more than a brother could be.

Instead of finding ways to make fun of him I spend my time watching him, but not in a creepy way. It's like I'm noticing him for the first time. All the things I didn't see years ago are now the only things I take notice of. Like the way his two front teeth show just a little as he parts his lips to smile or when he thinks really hard and the skin between his eyes at the top of his nose crinkles up in the cutest way. The minute I started noticing these things about him was the minute I knew I was crossing into forbidden territory. Now that's something that should be forbidden, unlike this amazing forest. However, I can't help the way I feel about him, even if I know it's wrong. I mean what if we did try to date and it ruined our friendship? What would I do then? The thought of losing our friendship is something I couldn't live with. He's always been the one constant thing in my life, the one thing to always keep my head above water. He's always been my rock, my everything and if that gets taken away it would be just as bad as if air stopped entering my lungs. He's the only reason I've survived this long in life so being without him isn't an option for me. So it's best not to stir the waters.

"Amberly."

I glance at Logan to see worry lines all over his young face, "Sorry, I'm doing it again."

"I've never seen you like this, is something going on?"

"No, really I'm fine."

He pauses for a brief moment before asking, "Is it because your birthday is getting close? I know how you don't like to celebrate it but don't let it get to you. Not this year. It's a big day."

Oh, man, he had to go and bring that up, like I didn't have enough on my mind already. Well, time to play it dumb, "Yeah, you caught me. And I know you're right, this is the year my powers mature and I can finally learn everything I've been begging my mother to teach me for longer than I can remember," I look deeper into the forest before I continue, "But it still doesn't change the fact of not having my father here with me, or feeling like something is missing. Turning eighteen is just something else he's missing."

"I know. I wish I could change that for you but sadly that's not one of the powers I have," I feel him staring at me as he takes in a deep breath, "I would take that from you in a heartbeat if I could."

I turn my gaze back in his direction not wanting to see on his face what I hear in his voice, but it's too late, I can see the hurt clear as day, "I know you would, I don't doubt that. And I'm sorry this was supposed to be a fun outing. A way for us to escape, even if only for a little while and I'm ruining it."

Logan forces a smile before he replies, "No, you're not I promise. But worrying about you is always going to be my job. I know you better than you think I do, and I know when something is hurting or bothering you."

"I know you do and I love that about you and about our relationship but it's not your 'job' to take care of me."

Now it's his turn to look off into the forest, "It may not be a job that was assigned to me, but it's one I chose a long time ago," he stops and looks down at me, "and for that reason alone it's more important. I'm always going to try to keep you happy." He pauses long enough to see the question in my eyes, "You and Troy are my family and I look out for my family, always."

And that answers that.

Logan looks at me one last time before he walks off after Troy. As I fall back behind the boys I notice that Troy's hair is getting too long. Normally his sandy blond hair would lie at his ears, but now it's down to his shoulders. The same goes for Logan's. He would always wear his dark raven hair so short that not one strand ever fell out of place but now the ends dangle just above his wide shoulder blades. Logan's the tallest one in our group, he easily towers over me and Troy. Troy being 6' and me being 5'6" and Logan being 6'3", they sure make a girl feel small. Being short is normal when you're a girl but man can it suck when someone like Troy tries to take something and keep it away from you, which he does to me daily. I can try to jump and get it out of his hands all day long and he will just stand there with a smile on his face mocking me. Just another thing that makes it easy for him to pick on me. Logan doesn't like being as tall as he is because he's very aware of his height and broad shoulders and often feels like people are afraid of him because of his size. I often catch him hunching over in front of new people, I think it's his way of trying to show he's not a threat but anyone who knows him knows how gentle he is and that he wouldn't hurt a fly unless there was a life or death situation going on. I think that's another reason why my feelings for him shifted. Men are normally hard or even mean at times, but Logan's always been kind and sweet, which most people tend to make fun of him for but for me it makes him more of a man than anyone else in our village.

I walk a little faster to close the distance between me and the guys but I stop dead after a few steps. Something feels off. It's the same feeling I get every time I come into these woods. I've felt it for years and it's one I can't seem to shake. But this time it feels different, more intense somehow.

I'm being watched. I look around the woods knowing there's someone lurking in them not far from where I'm standing. I can sense it's not someone from the village. It's hard to explain but everyone I know, every witch and warlock has a certain aura about them that can make it easy for me to know who's around me before my eyes even rest on them. It's a nice power to have because it lets me know if I'm in danger long before I am. So I know that this person who's watching me now is the same one who's been watching me for years and that it's not anyone in our village. I can also sense that they mean me no harm and maybe that's why I've kept it to myself all this time.

I turn back around to face the directions that the boys were going in but I don't see them. Before I get the chance to yell their names Troy steps from behind a tree with a wide grin on his face. I gasp and lift my hand to my heart.

"Did I scare you? Sorry, didn't mean to," he says as the grin on his face grows wider, "Oh, wait yeah I did."

Before I get the chance to tell him off I feel my chest growing hot under my hand. The heat is coming from the pendant around my neck, it was my mother's. It's the one thing she gave me that I never leave the house without. She gave it to me for my fifth birthday and I've worn it ever since. She told me when I turned thirteen that I needed to always wear it and never take it off, that it would protect me. I never really got to test that theory and hope I'll never get the chance to. I remember trying to ask my mother about the necklace many times but it was just another thing she wouldn't give me information about. I mean yeah sure wear the necklace, never take it off but God forbid you tell me anything about it. Like where it came from, what it's made of, and what it does. I know nothing about it but yet I wear it every day. But right now the amulet seems to think Troy's the threat. The one thing I did come to learn is when it gets hot there could be danger close by and the thought of it thinking Troy is a danger to me makes me smile as I think about him getting blasted on his ass. Growing up I only wore it because I wanted a way to be close to my mom, and I felt this amulet was the only way to do that. The older I got the more it grew on me and now it is like a second skin, I never leave the house without it. My favorite thing about it is that it changes colors. My mother says it does that based on not only my mood but also trouble. She said if it ever turns a bright orange I should get the hell out of dodge.

The stone is small enough to fit into the palm of my hand and its shape is rather odd. It's a circle with jagged edges and around the outside of the circle are three holes, like parts of the amulet are missing.

I remove my hand from the amulet as I see Logan walk up behind Troy, "Leave her alone. You're on another level today, man."

Logan walks over to me and puts his long, lean arm around my slim shoulder. He peers down at me, with his emerald eyes, and I become speechless as my heart skips another beat. It's a shame the amulet can't protect me from catching feelings that I shouldn't have.

Troy smiles, "Hey, I don't want to sit here, we came out to do something, didn't we? And I know it wasn't to flirt," Troy looks at Logan as he pulls his arm off my shoulder and walks over to him.

"So what do you have in mind?" Logan asks while running his thin long fingers through his raven hair.

Troy's grin grows as he looks my way. As his bronze-colored eyes find me he asks, "How about the game we played when we were twelve?"

I sigh, "That's a child's game."

"So, the loser has to sleep outside, what's not fun about that?"

I can see the distress on Logan's face but I turn my attention to Troy and say, "Sure why not, but who's it?"

"I'll do it since I was the one who suggested it. If I don't find either one of you in twenty minutes then I lose. Sound good?"

"Fine." I say in reply as I start to walk away from the boys, "But remember you asked for this when you're the one sleeping outside tonight."

Troy turns away next as Logan takes one last look at me then heads in a different direction to hide. I found a good spot inside a hole in a rotting old tree. It's very tall and still very healthy looking for a tree that's rotting out. Right outside from where I'm hiding I see a small river that I never noticed before.

The forest is such a beautiful peaceful place. The trees grow to be twice the size of houses and everywhere you look you can see rock like formations along the land. In some places there are even small mountains and the forest floor is bare with only dirt and rocks. In our village, we grow the crops and things we need for food but out here it's plain. It's hard for me not to see the beauty in this place that everyone else calls dangerous. If this is dangerous then call me crazy because there is no place I would rather be.

Time passes slowly as I wait for Troy to attempt to find me and I can't help but think about my mom. Our relationship is far from a normal one and it runs deeper than her just being closed off. I've felt like there's something she's been keeping from me and I've felt like this for longer than I can remember and sadly I think that's the main reason we are so distant from one another. I mean she's my mother. I want to have a relationship with her. I want us to be close but every time I try to get to know her or about our family, it's like she puts up this concrete wall around her, and no matter how hard I try I can't break it down.

The minutes continue to pass by but not fast enough. Squatting in this position is starting to make my back ache. As I continue to sit and wait, I decide it's time to get some answers. Tonight, when I get home I'm going to approach my mother and this time will be the last because tonight one way or another I'm getting some answers. I can't continue to live with all these questions about who I am and who our family is.

I hear the boys calling to me from a distance and I happily step out of the hole in the tree and begin to walk towards the direction that the boy's voices are coming from. I hear twigs break behind me and a grin creeps up on my face as I turn around. I look around for Troy but he's nowhere in sight. My smile fades as I turn back around to face the direction that I last heard the boy's voices come from and there, only five feet in front of me, stands a wolf.

Chapter 3

Logan

I yell her name one more time then look over at Troy, "Do you see her anywhere?"

He glances at the ground, "No, man. Don't see her."

I speak so low I know Troy has to strain to hear me, "Yeah, because she's not on the ground in front of your face man."

He scowls at me but doesn't say a word. I continue to sweep my eyes over the landscape in front of us but there's still no sign of her, "I know she heard us, so where is she?"

"Man, you know how she can be."

I turn on him fast and I know he can see the annoyance plastered across my face because he throws his hands up in surrender before saying, "Hey, I didn't mean anything bad by it. You know how she's always inside her head. Maybe she didn't hear us."

Looking back into the forest I say, "I know she heard us. Something isn't right."

"Dude, relax she's fine. We've been out here a million times before and there's nothing out here. Plus, she knows her way around these woods better than we do."

"Just because we haven't seen anything doesn't mean there isn't anything in these woods."

Troy releases a sigh, "OK, so let's say for argument's sake and came out after ten years of hiding and ran off with our little Amberly, what are you gonna do about it, man?"

I look back at him with a devilish grin plastered across my face, "I'll go hunting."

"Dude you are crazy." Troy puts his hand behind his head and rubs at the hair on the back of his neck as he starts to smile too. "But honestly she's fine I'm sure."

"I don't know. You know how she's good at finding trouble even when there's none to find."

Troy lets a laugh escape before replying, "Now that's very true. She can get in worse scraps than we can." Troy stops laughing and looks up at me with a straight look on his face before he continues, "But really man she can take care of herself, you should know that better than most."

A flashback takes residence in my head of the time she punched me in the jaw when we were only thirteen when I walked into her room as she was getting dressed. Troy's voice brings me back to reality when he says, "But man you have to stop getting so crazy worried about her all the time."

"What are you talking about? I worry about her just as much as I worry about you."

"Now who's lying?" He says as he wraps his arms over his chest, "Man the sad thing is you don't even see it."

Wanting to be done with this conversation I take off deeper into the woods. I hear Troy yelling for me to wait up but I tune him out. I can hear my breathing getting louder in my ears as I feel the cold ache in my lungs. But I won't stop. I'm running so fast that I don't see a tree's root sticking out of the ground until it's too late. I go flying. I lift my arms to cover my face as I meet the oncoming tree. The pain in my arm is excruciating but I push down the pain as I stand up. I wobble and find myself leaning against the tree for support. I guess the impact still got to my head despite my arm being in the way. I hear Troy in the distance continuing to shout my name.

Moron.

There are so many reasons why he shouldn't be yelling in the forest, not while he is by himself. Just because we've never seen anything that could be a danger to us doesn't mean there isn't something out here. We may be warlocks but we are still in training and there is only so much magic we can defend against.

I straighten myself and take a step. Then another. My balance is coming back to me again. I walk on slowly for a few minutes then pick up the pace. What if Troy had a point in what he said? What if I'm not seeing clearly? I mean he is right she can take care of herself, I've learned that firsthand. But maybe on some level, it's more than just worrying about her. When I'm not around her I want to be. I mean I've always wanted to be around her and always looked out for her well-being, but this feeling is something else. I look for danger where there is none and I look for excuses to just be around her. I mean we're friends, best friends and we've been close for almost eighteen years now and I can't let it become more than that and if Troy is seeing it then so will she. I have to get myself in check, and soon because the one thing I don't want to lose is her friendship, it means everything to me. She's gotten me through a lot of dark times and I don't know where I would be without her. So the thought of losing her is starting to make my heart ache because the thought is unbearable. We've always had each other and I don't want the day to ever come when we don't. So I need to get a hold of these feelings and bury them deep. I mean I've been doing it for the last ten years so what's another ten right?

I move around the tree in front of me and a small lake comes into view. As my eyes scan across the dirt-covered earth there's nothing in sight but trees, trees, and more trees. Worry is starting to settle in the pit of my stomach and that pit gets a whole lot bigger when my eyes come to rest upon a wolf. I slowly move back behind the tree, hoping it doesn't notice me. I peek around the side just enough to get a better view of the wolf, hoping there aren't more because this one is more than enough to worry about. He's huge. I've seen a lot of wolves in my years but this one has to be at least six foot in height and ten in length. I never knew a wolf could get that big or look that healthy in this forest for that matter. He's gotta weigh a few hundred pounds easily and his legs are long enough to reach where I stand in only a few strides. For a moment I consider the possibility that this wolf is one of the shifters from the other village. There are many others in the forest but theirs is the closest to ours and even that is a few day hike. But this wolf couldn't be a shifter, we have never seen one and from what we have been taught they hate our kind and keep their distance. So I doubt one would come all the way out here and alone for that manner. Either way, this one is huge and I may have full use of my magic but I am nowhere near ready to take on something that size.

Panic starts to set in and I know I need to get out of here before he notices I'm here but out of the corner of my eye I see something and turn to look in that direction and my heart stops.

Amberly.

Chapter 4

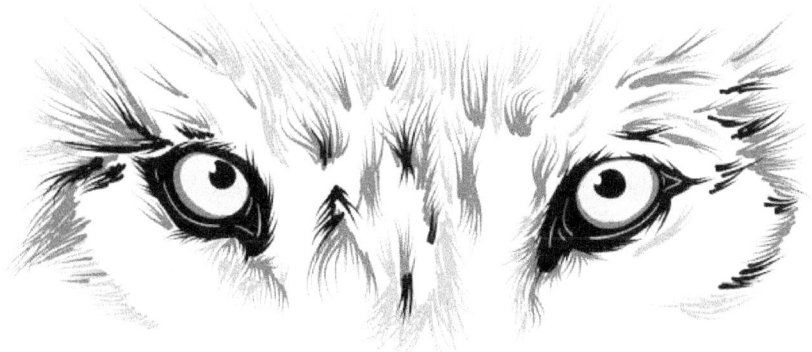

Amberly

The wolf is so close to me that I can see the whites of its eyes. His onyx colored coat shining in the moonlight throws me off guard.

For some reason I'm not as afraid as I was moments ago but I know I should be. I should be feeling nothing other than the need to run, to scream, but I feel nothing. No, that's a lie. I feel...

Safe.

He continues to stare at me and I'm dumbfounded. Wolves are supposed to have instincts that tell them to run the other way when there is danger and to a wolf, humans are just that, danger. So why is he sitting, and I mean sitting, here staring at me like he's studying me?

A noise sounds behind me and my fear kicks in. What if he's only been distracting me? What if this is some kind of game wolves play to catch their prey and what if that's another wolf behind me? All my training for this moment vanishes as I ready my body to make a run for it when a firm hand grabs my left arm. I turn to find Logan. He bends down slowly and whispers in my ear, "Don't move or he will charge us." I glance down at his free hand to find he's holding a butcher knife with a sharp serrated edge. One nice cut and you're a goner with that thing. My mind begins to wonder how he carried that all this whole time without me noticing. When I turn back to the wolf I find him now standing and bearing his teeth. A low growl escapes from his muzzle, and a moment later more wolves emerge from the forest behind him. Logan quickly moves around to get in front of me like a shield and that's when I hear it.

Stop! I mean them no harm, you can leave. I can handle it, he's only one human.

"What the hell?" I mumble.

I have to be losing my mind because there is no way I just heard a wolf talk because as far as I know, they can't. Can they? I've turned into a complete basket case. First, I think the wolf is analyzing me or something and now I think I can hear him talking. Man, I need some serious help when I get back home.

The wolf's attention returns to me and I swear he looks as surprised as I do. Then his eyes and muzzle change and I swear I see relief. I mean I can sense humans all day but I've never been able to communicate with an animal, no one in my village ever has. I look from the wolf to Logan and back again as they both continue to stare at me like I've lost my mind and then I realize why. I had spoken aloud.

You...understand me? The wolf's voice echoes through my mind.

Looking at him I hesitate, thinking before I try to answer. I think in my mind, *How is this possible?*

There are rumors among my pack, about our kind being intertwined. I've been interested in learning the truth for myself for some time. He takes a step forward and Logan stiffens next to me, *I wasn't sure if I would ever be able to get you alone.* He says while straightening his back.

Rumors? About what?

That's a story for another day. I came here to see if you would come back with me.

Questions begin forming in my mind so fast that I can't separate them. *Come back with you, where?*

I want to take you to my pack because I hope we can both get some answers there. Our alpha should be able to understand this.

Ignoring his answer I ask my next question as my mind needs time to process what he's saying. *Why did you come here because of a rumor? You're a wolf, humans are dangerous to you, plus the feud between all the supernatural villages. I don't understand why you would risk coming to look for someone you didn't know for a reason that makes no sense.*

He pauses for a minute to form what sounds like a sigh and then his voice echoes inside my head again. *I came because I had a feeling the rumors were true.*

I stifle a laugh as I reply, *You had a feeling? You based your safety on a feeling?*

The annoyance is clear in his voice when he says, *Well it was more than a feeling. I've sensed you for years, so after some time I came into the forest to search for you.* He pauses for a brief moment, maybe to collect his thoughts before continuing. *I've been watching you from a distance since we were both kids. I approached you today because you were separated from your,* He turned his gaze to Logan, *Men.*

The skin between my eyes scrunches together in confusion, *You sensed me? What does that even mean?*

Honestly, I'm not sure. One day I started feeling a pull. It felt like there was a magnet pulling me in this direction. Like I needed to find you for some reason and I couldn't stop until I did. But once I located you and learned I was being pulled by a human and a witch at that, I wanted to keep my distance and so I did for many years, until now.

My attention is pulled from our conversation as I glance at Logan. I can see him trying to think of a way out of the current situation we are in. He could use his powers but we were told to never use them against an animal unless it was absolutely necessary because our powers are connected with them as well as the universe. Right now the situation isn't calling for us to use them so he's trying to think of what to do next to make sure we don't have to use them. I hear something that sounds like a chuckle coming from the wolf. I turn my attention back to him reaching out with my mind. I ask, *What was that for?*

If a wolf could smile I would swear that right now that's what he was doing. *Nothing.*

Don't tell me nothing when that was clearly something. Why did you just chuckle?

He answers in a cocky tone *Because your human is rather funny.*

I try to ignore the human bit when I ask, *Funny? How?*

Because I can see him trying to think of a way out of this. So much so that I see steam coming from his ears.

Annoyed, I reply, *Don't make fun.*

I'm sorry, I can't help it, he's rather interesting to me.

My facial expression changes to one of confusion as I try to make myself understand. *Interesting how?*

I don't really know how to answer that question.

Sighing I say, *Fine then how about this one, why would a wolf feel a pull to me? Like you said, I'm human, I'm not like you.*

Well for starters I'm not a wolf I'm a human, well a shapeshifter to be more precise. At least that's what I've been told your kind would call us.

My mom told me about shapeshifters years ago. She had a bedtime story she would tell me often that had shifters in it but she also told me they had long since been extinct. As far as we all knew they were wiped out years ago, before I was even born. The more I would try to ask my mother about them the more she would pull away. I never understood why.

Ok, well that still doesn't explain why you would feel a pull to me. I'm not a shape shifter and I can't turn into a wolf so none of this is making any sense.

He looks at me with knowing eyes, *That's not necessarily true. Since you can communicate with me telepathically that means you can shift too, you just don't know it yet. It means you have shifter blood in your veins. That's also why I sensed you.* His eyes look around the forest to rest in the direction of my village. *You may live with them but you still have our blood inside you. There are rumors that many years ago some people from your home mated with ours and they had children. You may be a descendant of that bloodline.*

I take a quick look at Logan before I reply. *This is crazy. You're nuts, listen I don't know who you think I am or what you want from me but I'm sorry I can't help you. Whatever you came here for it was a waste of time.*

I understand that none of this is making sense to you now, I knew it wouldn't but I promise I can get you answers. All the questions you've had for years, the ones you keep asking but getting no answer for, I know someone who can give you what you have been searching for.

Overwhelmed, all I can get out is a question, *Can we please leave now?*

You've always been free to go, he says as he lies down, *but I'll be here waiting when you come looking for answers, and believe me you will.*

I turn away from the wolf and look at Logan, as all the wolves lie down in front of us. I grab Logan's arm and pull him with me as I take one last look at the black wolf.

"What are you doing, stop moving," Logan says as he pulls against me.

"It's OK we can leave now."

"What? Are you crazy? Stop moving, I'm going to get us out of this just give me another minute." He says, as his eyes continue to run over the many wolves lying on the ground.

I say in a low voice, "I'm not crazy. Please, just trust me we can go now."

Logan looks from me to the wolves one more time then pulls out of my grip to grab me by the arm, "Stay behind me."

We slowly make our way around the pack and back towards Troy and home. I hold Logan's hand the whole way as my mind buzzes with confusion. Tonight doors opened that I never knew were there in the first place and I fear now that they are they can never be closed. I know I need answers but the question now is who will I get those answers from? So much for thinking I had my life all figured out, talk about a page-turner.

Logan's hand in mine keeps me grounded. I'm so grateful to have him here with me, knowing he is the one constant thing in my life and that no matter where these doors lead he will always be by my side. He's always had a part of me, a part of my heart and so has my forest but now I fear the forest's call holds something different for me, and it's somewhere he can't follow, at least not yet. Once I get the answers I'm looking for I will share everything with him but until then I need to keep this a secret. I don't need him asking questions that I don't have the answers to.

I see Troy waiting for us off in the distance and the look of relief is evident on his face. As we close the distance between us I hear a high pitched cry coming from the trees. I know in my heart it's the wolf calling to me and surprisingly I find myself wishing I could answer his call.

Chapter 5

Amberly

My mind is plagued with so many thoughts since returning home from the forest. But one in particular keeps crawling its way to the surface. I want to go back into the forest. There is still so much I need to know and the answers are on the other side of these walls. Everyone in my village knows what happened today with the wolf. The moment we re-entered the village everyone was all over us. Apparently, my mother had been looking everywhere for me. So the moment my feet landed on the chestnut color soil of our home all eyes were on us. It didn't help that Troy is a loudmouth and can't keep a secret to save his life, at least when it comes to my mother. He won't admit it but I know he's afraid of her. So now no one is allowed outside the gates. Yes, we weren't supposed to go out before but now everyone in the village is watching me to make sure I stay inside these walls. I wish Troy could learn to keep his mouth closed.

The only thing I do know for sure is there's something my mother isn't telling me and I've known it for years. I always wondered who my father was, but she wouldn't tell me. I even asked around the village once but no one said a word and now I know why. Maybe, the wolf was telling the truth. Maybe my father is part wolf, or maybe he was at least a descendant of the shifters.

I leave my hut and start down the dirt-covered walkway to Logan's. I take note of the laundry washing itself in our backyard washing well, I guess mom put a load on. I pause and watch as a pair of my teal slacks ring themselves out over the garden and then lay themselves on the long, overly used clothes line that wraps one end around a nearby tree and the other from the side of our hut. It's nice to not have to worry about things like laundry like the other villages around here. Magic saves you time on the simple things. We use it to do the wash, clean dishes, and straighten messes around the house. Most of the time we can use our minds and the magic flows other times we have keywords for certain spells. Few witches and warlocks need wands but others that are from a strong bloodline, like me, Troy and Logan, we don't need them. With a wave of the hand or strong thoughts, there isn't much we can't do. It's simply learning how to control the power and learning the spells.

Walking down the path that leads from my hut to Logan's I see that a few of our crops are coming into season as they pluck themselves from the earth and drop into separate baskets labeled sweet eats, diet herb, honey, lemons, apples, and peaches. The new *'Growth Spell'* spell my mom came up with is working beautifully because these were just planted in the garden last night.

There's so much we can do and so much I still need to learn. I know a few simple protection potions, spells and some self defense moves. Mom thought it best to start with those but I don't get the purpose since no one ever really enters the village and I'm never supposed to leave it. Logan and Troy have also been teaching me a few things on the side since my mom wants to focus on other things. So now I'm also covered in light levitation, which is kind of like floating or flying, as well as telekinesis, which really just means I can move things with my mind when I focus hard enough. I've also noticed I have other powers but I've been too afraid to say anything.

I'm pretty sure I can read people's minds. There was this one time when Logan and I went to the market to get my mom a few things for dinner and we were walking in silence. I heard someone say "What's Midnight doing out?" Midnight is a cat that likes to sneak out of our neighbor's house and roam the village. The person's voice sounded like Logan's but when I looked at him he was silent but his eyes were focused on the cat. Then a moment later he walked up to Midnight and picked him up in his arms and said those same words and that's when I knew I must have heard the thought as he said it in his mind. However, that's not the scariest thing I've learned I can do. I'm pretty sure I can tell the future and have visions as well. Now, other than my mom, only a handful in our village have different gifts from the rest, but I never thought I would be one of them. Not knowing what you can really do can be a scary thing.

The walk from my hut to Logan's isn't too far so before I know it I'm standing in front of him. I climb the ladder to the upper half of Logan's hut, which is where he tends to spend all his free time. I reach the top but stop in my tracks. I feel like maybe I shouldn't be here. I know he has a lot that he is dealing with and I don't want to add to those problems. It's bad enough that I'm sure my mother is going to yell at him later for us being out in the forest. She always makes him accountable for the things I do wrong like he's my keeper, which is beyond annoying. Then there's also what happened. I want to tell him the whole truth but what if I do and he thinks I'm crazy? I don't think I could handle that. I mean how do you tell anyone, let alone your best friend, that you can telepathically communicate with wolves?

"Hey, there you are," I look up to see Logan standing in front of me.

"Hey. Were you looking for me?" I feel something hot and wet running down my finger so I look back down at my hands and realize that I have been picking away at my cuticles and now I've made one bleed.

Logan follows my gaze and sees the blood.

"You need to stop doing that when you get nervous." He says as he grabs me lightly around the wrist and pulls me into his hut. When we get inside he makes me sit down while he looks around for something. "So what were you worrying about now?" He says as he turns back around only for a second to look at me.

"What makes you think I was worrying about anything?" I smile at him and then look back at my finger.

"Because I know you, when you worry you fidget." He picks up a towel and bowl and walks over to where I'm sitting. He places the towel down next to me and takes the bowl over to the sink and begins to fill it with water.

Although we live in huts we still have plumbing and electricity in our homes. We may not have the more modern look like the humans do in their cities and suburbs but this is how we prefer to live. Being in the forest a hut feels more at home than sheetrock and concrete walls.

"I don't know. I didn't realize I was worrying about anything." He grabs the now full bowl of water and kneels in front of me. He takes my hand in his and begins to wipe at the blood and dirt softly. Avoiding the cut the best he can. "You don't have to do that, I can do it."

He looks at me through his long dark bangs. His hair just touches his shoulder, long enough to run my hand through. His eyes are always full of love when he looks at me but I know that love is for his friend and nothing more. However, his face is currently wearing a look I've only seen on him once before when he gazed at a girl named Lily, we were twelve years old. He told me she was his first crush. But why would he stare at me with that same look he gave her? He doesn't have those feelings towards me, does he?

30

"I know you can but I want to do it for you." He looks back down and finishes cleaning the cut as gently as he can. When he's done he puts the bowl and the dirty towel in the sink to clean later. I stand up and take a step towards him and trip over one of his sandals that he left in the middle of the floor. I almost fall on my face but Logan, with his fast reflexes, catches me right before I hit the ground. I'm about to say thank you but when I look into his eyes no words come out.

The thoughts I had earlier about him seep into my brain as I stand here in his arms. Today it feels different, we feel different. I can feel it in his touch that something has changed, but I don't know what and I don't know when this change took place. Logan has always been protective of me and always been there to catch me when I fall, literally, but I never noticed till now how many times that has been.

Why would he bother wasting all his time and effort on me if he didn't want more than friendship? I mean yes, of course he would be there for me as a friend but as much as he has been, I don't think so. Maybe I'm reading too much into it. I try to pull away from him but his broad arms are firm around me, even as I try to remove myself they stay firmly in place.

I can feel the muscles in his arms under mine as I look deeper into his eyes. His hands grow tense on my back and I can see in his face that he is thinking hard about something. Before I get the chance to ask what it is he moves a strand of my auburn hair away from my face. Just as quickly as his hand was there it was gone again and before I even had time to register what was going on he was away from me and across the room.

I take one step towards him and pause, not sure what to say. Then I hear Troy's annoying voice through the fog in my brain.

"Hey, Logan what's taking you so…Oh, I see," Troy looks at me and smiles.

Logan turns to look at Troy fast, and he almost looks mad, "Sorry, I forgot we were supposed to help your mom today. I didn't realize it was that late already. Can you give me a half hour? I have a few things I need to do first."

Troy looks from Logan to me and his smile returns, "Yea, sure no problem. See you in a few."

Then he walks out the door and leaves me and Logan alone in the silence.

I turn to walk out too but then Logan is standing in front of me.

"Was there some reason you stopped by?" Logan asks.

"I...no I just wanted to see what you were getting into tonight. But it seems you already have plans with Troy," I release a small laugh that sounds more like a groan, "So I'll see you later then?"

As I walk out the door I hear Logan's low reply coming from behind me, "Sure. See you later."

Chapter 6

Amberly

"Nice job breaking the guy's heart and right after he saves your ass from the wolves nonetheless."

Heat rushes to my cheeks as I stare at Troy angrily. I continue walking towards the front gate, "You don't know what you're talking about. Why don't you go back home and wait for him there," I picked up the pace, feeling the need to get outside.

"Where are you going in such a hurry?"

"It's none of your business. How about you go and bother someone else?" I can hear the hatred in my voice and it almost makes me wince.

"No, I like bothering you." He says with a smile on his face.

I try not to let him annoy me but that's what Troy knows how to do best. The smile on his face starts to dissipate when we reach the gate. As I grab for the lock Troy's hand goes around my wrist and I look up at him as I pull out of his grasp.

"What are you doing? You can't go out there, not after what happened." He says while freeing me.

"I can do whatever I want." I lift my chin and look at the lock again.

"I don't think your mom or Logan would like this very much." He looks down at me with a smile while he reaches for me again.

"Then why don't you run off and tell them?"

Troy raises his hands in surrender, "Hey, come on now you know I didn't have a choice."

If looks could kill I'm sure he would have dropped right at my feet, "Yes, you did and you chose wrong."

"Hey, come on, just talk to me. I know you prefer talking to Logan but I'm just as good."

I cross my arms over my chest and look away from him. "I don't want to talk about anything."

"You forget I know you just as well as Logan does. I know something is bothering you." He pauses, and takes a step closer to me before he continues, "Since we got back you've been quieter than normal. Come on, tell me what's wrong."

I remain silent.

Realization becomes plain on his face as he says, "Fine don't talk to me but I want you to know it's OK."

Intrigued, I can't help but answer. "What's OK?"

The sunlight hits his eyes and I can see all the different shades of bronze in them as he replies, "To be scared or affected by what happened."

Annoyed, I bellow back at him as I throw my arms to my side, "Afraid! I wasn't afraid. You don't know what you're talking about Troy." I pause for a moment to take in a slow breath, trying to calm myself down before continuing. "Stop trying to understand because you'll never understand. It has nothing to do with that. It's something so much more and there's no way to explain it, or at least not right now."

Hurt shines in his eyes at my words and I almost feel bad as I turn away again. I need to get out of here, my mother isn't going to give me any answers so I need to go get them myself and I need to go now. If I wait until I talk to my mother I'll never get out of here.

I reach for the gate again and this time Troy grabs me around the waist and begins to drag me backward. "What the hell are you doing? Let me go!," I practically screamed at him.

"Sorry, but I can't let you go out there, you're right I don't know what's going on with you but I'll be damned if I let anything happen to you." Troy tightens his hold around me as I squirm. He never stops pulling me away from the gate saying, "You'll thank me later."

Without a second thought, almost as if my body worked without my brain telling it to, I lift my elbow, high and bring it down fast until I feel it connect with his stomach, and at the same moment I throw my head back until it hits his nose with a sickening crunch and he releases me.

Troy's hands go to his face as he falls to the ground and says, "What the fu-. Amberly, you could have broken my nose."

While he's on the ground I make a run for it. I look back at him, for only a second, to see him bent over and wobbling. I would be lying if I didn't say I felt a little bad for possibly breaking his nose, but then again he kind of deserved it after all these years.

I turn back to the gate, and stretch out my hand, thinking hard I say, "Apertus!" The lock breaks open with a bang.

The minute I get my body through the opening I make a run for it. I can hear Troy calling my name in the distance but I keep going and I don't stop again until I can't breathe. When I think I'm far enough away I sit down on the ground and lean my back against a tree. Taking shallow breaths and slowing my heart rate.

I close my eyes and clear my mind. *Wolf, are you there?*

My name isn't Wolf, it is Julian. The familiar voice says with a little chuckle.

I open my eyes to find the large raven-coated wolf in front of me. *Where is the rest of your pack?*

I don't need them here so I sent them home. He looks at me and yawns. *So, you called?*

Yes, I need answers. I say with a pleading voice. I wish I didn't sound so needy. *You said if I went with you, you could get them for me. I need to make sense of all of this and I know I won't get that in there.* I nod my head in the direction of my home.

I look at the wolf for a moment before what looks like a smile forms on his muzzle. Come *with me and I will answer all of your questions. And whatever I can't answer they can.*

Who are they?

The wolf, or should I say, Julian, begins to stand before he answers, *You'll see.* He turns around to expose his backside to me. *Are you coming?*

I hesitate for a moment before asking, *How do I know I can trust you?* A part of me knows logically that I shouldn't go anywhere with him but how else will I learn the truth?

I didn't attack you earlier and neither did the rest of my pack. He shifts his body and I can tell he's becoming a little impatient. *We don't have much time; your humans are on their way you must decide.*

Where will we be going?

To my pack, I promise no harm will come to you and you will get your answers there.

I look off towards my home before turning my back on it and moving towards the wolf, knowing that my answer was made long before I re-entered the forest, *I need to know.*

Julian moves to stand in front of me. *Get on.*

What? Are you crazy? I look at him with a mix of disbelief and uncertainty. *We will move faster this way.*

I stare at Julian, unsure of how to proceed.

With a grin he says, *Just grab on and pull yourself up. You can't hurt me.*

I hesitate for a second before gripping fistfuls of his fur and pulling myself up and over onto his back. Once in place, he takes off at full speed into the forest with my fingers tangled in his fur.

Chapter 7

Logan

As I walk out of my hut I find Troy wobbling in the dirt. I ran over to him, placing his arm around my shoulders before walking him over to a stone.

"What happened? Your nose is bleeding." I stare at him in horror. Who could have done this to him? Not anyone in the village.

Troy mumbles something from behind his hand.

"What?" I ask.

He moves his hand away from his face so I can hear him better, "Amberly."

My eyes widen as I stand and look around, "What about her? Is she OK, where is she?"

Troy grabs my arm and pulls me back down to him, "She did this to me."

Shock forms over my face, "What? No, Amberly, wouldn't do that."

"Yes, she would. If I was trying to stop her from something she wanted badly enough," He looks up at me through his mangled hair.

I look away before answering, "And what is it she wanted?"

"I think you know," as he looks at me I can see the color around his nose and eyes darkening, "Where does she always run when she needs to escape from life here?"

I look toward the forest and sigh.

* * *

As Troy and I walk into Amberly's hut I make out her mother's silhouette. Mrs. Grayson has been through a lot over the years just like her daughter. No one knows very much about what happened and she won't talk about it. The village believes that after she became pregnant her family and husband went into the forest in an attempt to find food to last the winter and they never returned. As far as everyone knows Amberly and her mother are the only ones left in their family.

Mrs. Grayson turns around with a smile, "I was wondering when you would get home Amber..." Even in the dark I can see how much her face fell when she realized it wasn't her daughter. I knew they had been fighting a lot, but I don't know what about.

Mrs. Grayson looks away from us and says, "Hi, boys how are you today?"

Troy takes a step closer and I stop him with my arm. I look at him once and then back to Mrs. Grayson, "We...I need to talk to you. It's important."

She turns around to face me and a smile creeps onto her face, "Oh, Logan. I'm so happy for you both."

The next thing I know she's across the room and embracing me. I look over at Troy and see shock and confusion on his face as he raises his hands shrugging his shoulders.

"Mrs. Grayson, what do you think I have come here to talk about?"

She lets go of me and looks up to meet my eyes, "Why the proposal of course, what else is there?"

She must see the shock form on not just my face but Troy's as well, for her face turns blank. "Or maybe I am wrong. I could have sworn. Do you not love my daughter?"

The question throws me so far off course that I don't know what to say. I hear Troy's voice come from behind me, "There is something of more importance that we need to tell you first. You see your daughter has-"

"Yes, I do." I hear the words come out of my mouth before I can stop them.

Troy throws his hand over his eyes as he shakes his head. A moment later he winces and withdraws his hand and I think this is the first time Mrs. Grayson really looks at Troy as her facial expression turns to one of concern. She walks over to him and takes his chin in her hand. Turning his face side to side gently before asking a little angrily, "Who did this to you?"

Troy smiles before answering, "I'm not too sure you want to know the answer to that question."

Taken aback by his answer she removes her hand and takes a step back. "Troy, tell me who did this to you."

"If you insist, just remember I warned you."

Her impatience is evident as she wraps her arms over her chest and starts to tap her foot lightly. She may only be a few inches over five feet but man she can be scary.

Troy looks at me out of the corner of his eye before he continues. "Your daughter."

Mrs. Grayson's arms go limp at her sides before she says in disbelief, or maybe I should say denial since this isn't the first time Amberly has punched someone. "My daughter did this to you? But why?" Troy goes to open his mouth but she silences him when she raises a hand and asks, "What did you do this time, Troy?"

Hurt written all over his face he says, "I didn't do anything," Troy can see the disbelief on Mrs. Grayson's face so he pauses before adding, "This time. I didn't do anything this time."

"Ok, then what happened?"

"Well, you see."

Sweat begins dripping off Troy as he struggles with what to say next, so I walk over and put a hand on his shoulder and say, "Amberly, was heading for the gate and Troy tried to stop her, and as a result she did this to him." I gesture to his nose then continue, "She's gone. She ran into the forest and I was coming here to let you know I'm going after her."

Chapter 8

Logan

"I'll find her." Was all I could say as I walked out of the hut with Troy on my heels. I look at him and frown, "Glad to see that was entertaining for you?"

"I thought she had the right to know her daughter went off on her own and will most likely end up dead."

My hands form into fists at my sides. I would love to hit him right now but I know that won't help matters, plus I would definitely break his nose, if it wasn't already broken. "Well the least you could have done was be the one to come out and tell her then, but no, instead you make me tell her."

"Well, why not. I mean she likes you so she can't get mad at you. However, she can't stand me. If I told her, I would have had to deal with some kind of punishment, I'm sure."

I can't help but laugh at him, "Amberly, wasn't kidding. You are afraid of her mom."

"Man, you're crazy not to be."

I look at Troy and notice his nose has almost doubled in size, man she got him good. "Maybe I just have no reason to be afraid of her. Just because she's in charge of the village doesn't mean she would ever do anything to hurt us, so there's no reason to be afraid. It's logic really."

"Or we can just toss it up to your lack of survival skills."

Choosing to ignore him I turn to the forest, "Trust me I'm the sane one out of the two of us and my survival skills are much better than yours," I pause and say in the next breath, "I'm going after her."

"You think I don't know that already and you should already know I'm coming with you," Troy says with a smile.

"Wipe that grin off your face."

"If I must." He says as a frown takes its place.

Troy and I walk in silence to the hole in the gate. I lift it up to allow him to pass first but he pauses and looks at me, "What if we don't find her? Or worse, what if she's…"

"She's not. I would know if she was. I would feel it. Plus, like you said, she knows how to handle herself."

I don't know why she went out there on her own but I will find her.

Chapter 9

Amberly

The night wind feels good on my hot skin. Julian is running so fast that it feels like needles against my flesh but I welcome the feeling.

It's hard to describe this; it's like nothing I've ever experienced before. He's running so fast that everything we pass looks like a blur and it makes me wonder how he can see anything.

We've been traveling for what feels like forever but it couldn't have been more than a few hours. However, I do know it's been some time because I'm getting sleepy and I'm losing feeling in my fingers from holding his fur so tight for so long.

As if in response Julian says, *We can stop for the night if you would like.* *How much longer till we get there?*

He pauses for a moment, maybe to think, then says, *Well I've been running for about three hours now but the whole trip to my pack is at least a day's run.*

Surprised that we are still so far away from our destination I can't form a reply so taking my silence as his answer he begins to slow.

We will stop here for the night. We both could use the rest.

He lies down to let me off and I'm so tired that when my feet touch the ground I almost fall over and I would have if it weren't for Julian. He uses his mouth to lightly grab onto my shirt to steady me. *Thank you.*

He opens his mouth to release me and then looks away. Maybe it's from lack of sleep but for the first time I really look at him and I can't help but think how beautiful he is. I've never been this close to a wolf before but this is something else. Knowing he's not just a wolf but a human almost trapped inside a wolf's body makes this experience so different. I wonder what he looks like as a human. If it's anything like his wolf I'm sure he's beautiful.

I hear Julian stifle a laugh and that's when I remember that my thoughts aren't my own. *I have a question.*

I'll do my best to answer it.

I have many questions but I think this is a good one to start with. *Can you only hear my thoughts when in wolf form or will you still be able to hear them when you're human too?*

Normally, it's only when you're in wolf form that you can telepathically speak to others of your kind.

I let out a sigh, *Well, that's good.*

Julian chuckles, *And why is that?*

It would kind of suck to always have to watch my thoughts around a room full of shapeshifters.

The night breeze picks up and as the cold night air hits my skin, I shiver involuntarily. Julian takes notice and without a word he stands up and walks over to where I am now sitting. He brushes himself against me making sure to wrap himself and his warm fur all around my body before lying down in the spot next to me. *You can lean against me if you're tired. I won't bite.*

Thankful that he offered before I have to ask I lean back and look up at the night sky, *So what else can you do?*

Well, you already know about being able to change form and telepathy and speed. We are also very strong and have great hearing.

Does any of it work in human form or is it just when you're a wolf?

He looks up at the sky before he says, *Everything other than the telepathy we can do in human form as well.*

The questions just keep coming and without any thought, I ask my next ones, *So how does it work? What I mean is at what age did you start to be strong or hear things from far away or how old were you when you first shifted?*

Julian looks down to the dirt covered earth, trying to collect his thoughts for his answer I suppose. He turns his head to look me in the eyes before replying, *Everyone is different so that is a hard question to really answer, however, for me I was five when I started to notice that I could hear things that were a great distance away. And I was twelve when I shifted for the first time. As for how it works, that's even harder to describe. It's kind of like you focus really hard on seeing yourself shift and you just do it. After the first few times, you get used to it and don't need to focus as hard.*

How did you learn to shift? I pause, afraid to ask the next question, *and does it hurt?*

I can tell he doesn't really want to answer but he makes himself when he says, *A friend taught me how to. Normally, it's your parents who teach you but mine died when I was very young. As for it hurting, again that is different for each person.*

I see I hit a sore subject and decided it's time to change the subject, *So how come I haven't shifted or been able to hear things from great distances if I'm like*

46

you?

Julian lays his head down on his big paws, *That I don't know.*

Do you think I'll get all the answers when we get to your pack?

Yes. If anyone can give you answers, it's Aaron. Now go to sleep we have a long day ahead of us.

The skin between my eyes crinkles up as I ask, *Who's Aaron?*

I didn't know it would be possible to see annoyance on a wolf's face but there it is plain as day. I raise my hands in submission as I say, *Alright, alright I'm going to bed.* I lay my head down on his fur and begin to drift. I didn't realize how tired I was until this second. Within minutes I'm fast asleep.

* * *

I wake up to the smell of fresh fruit. I open my eyes to find Julian lying five feet away from me as he looks off into the distance. The sun is already high in the sky and the heat beating down on me is making me so hot I want to strip. I sit up and start to stretch when Julian takes notice and turns around to look at me.

How did you sleep?

Puzzled, not yet used to hearing someone else in my head, I jump before I can form an answer, *I slept OK, you should have gotten me up though.*

I didn't mean to scare you.

I reach for a piece of fruit before I realize he isn't saying anything else so I reply, *It's not your fault it's just going to take some time for me to get used to hearing someone else in my head.*

Sorry, for me, normally, I have to remind myself that this is all new to you. I haven't been around anyone other than my pack so that part is new for me.

I take a bite of the peach that Julian found for me and the taste is overwhelming. We have peaches in my village but nothing as juicy as this one. I swallow before I say, *Seems we both have some things to get used to. So how did you sleep?*

Julian stands and stretches, *Sleep was fine. You should finish that so we can start our day. It's going to be a long one.*

I quickly eat the rest of the peach knowing I want to get to the cave before I need to sleep again. The peach was so juicy that it was all over my hands so I wiped them on my clothes as I heard a rustling sound coming from behind me. I turn around to see what it is, and there, breathing in my face is a bronze-colored wolf. I can feel the heat of his breath on my skin and before I can react Julian is there pushing me to the side with his body. He bends down on his front legs growling at the new wolf.

A moment later I hear him in my head, *Get behind me and don't move.*

Without another word I take a few steps backwards to give him some room, praying he won't need it. The bronze wolf's gaze comes back to me and Julian stands up tall before growling again. The other wolf turns his attention to Julian, I guess finally realizing he would have to deal with him first.

I stifle a grasp when the wolf opens his mouth and lunges towards Julian. Thankfully he moves fast enough to avoid its teeth. In return, Julian bounces up on his back legs and brings his body down hard on the wolf. He reaches around and brings his teeth down on the back of the other wolf's neck as it releases a vicious cry and tries to shake Julian off. When that doesn't work the wolf starts to back up to the nearest tree with Julian still on its back. When it gets within two feet of its destination I realize what it's going to do so I say in my mind to Julian, *Jump now!*

Surprised, Julian lets go and jumps off the wolf just as he lifts himself and slams his back into the tree right where Julian was only a second ago. The wolf cries out as it falls to the ground. It picks itself back up slowly and growls as it looks from Julian to me and back again. Realizing he can't win he turns away and runs back into the forest.

Julian stares after him for a few minutes before returning his attention to me, *Are you alright?*

Am I alright? You're the one who just went up against the wolf, not me.

Julian's muzzle forms into a smile before he says, *We should really get going. I don't know if he will be coming back.* He leans down to let me on his back and once I've got a good enough grip on his fur he stands back up.

Before continuing on our way he turns around to look at me, *And thank you by the way.*

It takes me a second to realize that he's thanking me for warning him about the tree. *We make a pretty good team.*

Julian turns his attention back to the forest before saying, *Seems we do.* Then he takes off at a faster pace than last night. So fast I lean my body down to where every inch is touching his fur.

* * *

Julian

Every bone in my body is starting to ache but we aren't much further from the cave so I keep pushing on. I forgot how long of a journey it was from my village to hers and I can tell this is the longest trip she's ever been on. Just minutes ago I could feel her holding onto my fur but now her arms dangle at my sides and I know she has fallen asleep. I slow my pace to one where she won't slide and fall off but I'm determined to get home before she wakes up.

It's a weird feeling being around her. A part of me wants to drag this out and just be alone with her, but another part wants to get as far away from her as possible. This feeling is unsettling and something I've never felt before. You would think it was something I've gotten used to over all these years but for some reason since I've been this close to her it's only gotten worse, stronger. When I look at her all I want to do is protect her and be with her every second and there is no such thing as too close, it's more like I'm never close enough.

She's a plain-looking kind of girl but yet she's so beautiful. The way her wavy elbow-length auburn hair curls around her body like it's a shield protecting her and the way her brown hazel eyes shine even in the darkest of places is what makes her stand out to me but so does her strength. She's a very slim girl, so slim I'm worried she would break easily but at the same time she's so strong. I've seen her grow over the years and seen her become this fiercely independent woman. She doesn't give up easily and she always gets her way no matter what she needs to do to get it. She's like no other girl I've ever met and maybe that's why I feel this connection to her because she reminds me of myself.

She starts to shift on my back and I know she's going to wake up soon so I run faster and shake my head to get the thoughts of her out of my mind. Once the cobwebs clear I look straight ahead and feel the dirt covered earth under my paws and smile as I pick up the pace and run faster than I ever have in my life. With only one destination on my mind, home.

Chapter 10

A mberly

Julian stops to let me off his back but I pause long enough to ask, "How much further?"

We're here, Julian says as he shakes his flank, as I fall to the ground he steady's me with his body.

I take a look around at my surroundings. I've never been this deep into the forest before and I'm sure if I tried to find my way back I would get lost.

I'd be lying if I didn't say that thought scares me. I feel a chill in my bones as a shiver escapes from the center of my body.

Julian walks away from me and into the large cave that stands in front of us.

The cave is the biggest one I've ever seen. It's as tall as the highest tree and wider than my whole village. The trees around here are tall but have long pointy looking needles on them instead of leaves and the earth floor has many patches of grass and bolder clusters.

Are you coming?

I turn to see Julian reemerge from the cave entrance. I come to rest my eyes on him and nod my head as I slowly follow behind him and enter the dark cave.

* * *

Amberly

"He will be back soon." The girl sitting next to me says. She told me her name was Angela. It's strange knowing everyone in here is a wolf. Although I can't call her a wolf, I guess because she's sitting next to me as human as I am.

When I entered the cave Julian disappeared and Angela was the only person I saw. She told me she was a wolf and everyone else here was too but the deeper into the cave I went there were still no wolves in sight, only humans. Everyone here can turn into a wolf. I feel, almost, jealous. What it must be like to be able to run through the woods and feel the dirt under your paws and not your feet, that thought is rather welcoming to me.

However, I will be the first to admit that Angela looks different, and when I say different I mean in a human way. Her eyes are a color I have never seen before. They are a mix of yellow, brown, and blue. The yellow is a deep dark color like the moon and the brown and blue colors are light in her eyes. Most of the people here have the same color eyes. Her elbow-length hair is the dark color of a raven but it has turquoise and lemon streaks running through it. I think of asking her how she got her hair that way but then she opens her mouth and I don't want to interrupt her.

"Julian, says you came here for answers."

I try not to look bewildered when I reply, "Yes, and honestly I don't even know what question to start with. So much has changed and the only thing I know is that I can talk to wolves."

A smile creeps onto Angela's face. "That honestly doesn't surprise me because I could sense it the moment you entered the cave."

I can't hide my surprise when I ask, "What does that mean?"

"It means that you are one of us." She replies.

"So you're saying I'm like you and Julian? That I can turn into a wolf too?"

"Yes, with the proper training, you'll be able to in no time."

I look down to see my cuticle bleeding not realizing I was picking at it. That's a habit I need to kick soon. Intrigued, I ask, "Is that what you did? You were trained to learn how to shift too?"

Angela's face contorts with what I think is pain as she looks away from me I know I've hit a nerve but I don't know what I asked that was wrong and not too sure what to say to remove that look from her face, "I'm sorry. I didn't mean to pry."

The smile starts to make a slow reappearance as she turns to face me once more. "It's fine. It's just a long story."

"Well, I'm a good listener if you ever want to talk about it."

The smile is now fully formed on her face as she looks around the cave to see who is listening or maybe to see who is around. I don't know which. But when she turns back to face me she looks like herself again, or at least the one I met when I first entered the cave.

"I'm not originally from this pack. Aaron saved me."

I try not to look confused as I ask, "Saved you how?"

"I was left for dead by my pack in the woods when I was only ten years old. I've been with Aaron for almost eleven years now."

I ask the easiest question first, "So you're almost twenty-one?"

"Yes. How old are you?"

I sigh as I reply, "Too young."

Angela is quiet for a long time so I know I need to start the conversation back up if I want to understand what happened to her. "So why did they leave you there?"

Her face falters again but it only takes a moment for her to correct herself. "There was an attack in our village. I don't remember much because I was young and it was many years ago but what I do remember is more like a nightmare than anything else." She pauses for a minute to take a deep breath. "Humans killed my whole family but they weren't your normal kind of humans. They didn't have powers like you do either but they had these weapons that power emerged from. I remember watching as bolts of what looked like lightning swept through my whole village and in the wake of that bright white flame laid my family. The ones who got away went deeper into the forest."

She went quiet again so I decided to ask another question. "How did you get here? I mean after all that how did you survive?"

I can see she's trying to recall the memory before she replies, "I'm not one hundred percent sure how but I do remember someone grabbing me by the back of the shirt and pulling me through the bushes."

"Is that all you remember?"

Her face goes to work harder as the lines around her eyes and lips deepen in thought. "I remember it was a man, maybe my father. He picked me up and then dropped me in the bushes a little way out from our village. A few days passed and I was in and out of consciousness and very dehydrated and that's when Aaron found me," she pauses but only for a moment to smile, "If it wasn't for him I would be dead. I owe him everything, including my life."

I try to put myself in her shoes, try to imagine losing everyone I've ever known, ever loved and the thought cripples me. I want to ask more but I'm taken aback when Angela raises her hand to wipe the tear from her face and I see a light pink scar just under the cuff of her sleeve. Without even thinking I grab her arm and pull the sleeve up to look, she doesn't stop me or pull away, and to my surprise, I've seen this before.

"Where did you get this?"

With confusion in her voice, Angela says, "I was born with it. Why?"

"Have you ever met anyone else who had the same mark?"

As if it wasn't a weird question at all she answers, "Actually, yes. A young man named Cole and his twin sister Celine had the same mark. They were born with it too."

"Were they from your village?"

Her answer almost sounds like a question when she says, "Yes."

"Did they by any chance make it out with you?"

I can see the sadness returning to her face and it pains me but I must know everything she does, "I don't think they could have made it out of there alive."

"I'm sorry I don't mean to be insensitive but did they happen to say anything about this scar? Did they know anything about it?"

The confusion returns as she smiles and says, "No, we didn't talk about it like that. They thought it was pretty cool how we all had the same birthmark, or scar as you call it." A look crosses her face, she looks intrigued as she continues, "Why so interested?"

I can't seem to form any words so instead I lift my shirt to show her the skin on my side right near my breast and I hear her suck in a deep breath before saying, "How is that possible? That looks almost exactly like mine."

I put my shirt back down to cover the birthmark that has forever intrigued my interest. I never understood how a birthmark could look like this. It's almost the size of a tennis ball in shape but it looks like a bird when you look close enough at it. However, I did notice one main difference between Angela's and mine. Yes, they are both the same size, shape, and even animal, but mine has five circular rings behind it that are all intertwined with one another but two that are next to each other are darker than the rest, whereas hers looks more like flames.

I remember she asked me a question and I did my best to get back to our conversation, replying, "I don't know, but you're not the first person I've known to have it either. I find it a little nerve-wracking if I am honest. I mean how can two different people, who have never met before, be born with the same birthmark?"

Before she can answer an unfamiliar voice calls her name from behind me.

I turn to see a man much older than Angela. He looks like he has to be around my mother's age. I can see the gray starting to creep into the sides of his shoulder-length hair; the rest is a raven color like mine but has a tint of emerald running through it. His eyes are different too. They are unlike the rest of the packs. They are the color of tangerines instead of yellow and onyx instead of brown. The only color that remains the same as the rest of the pack, is the blue. He's also much bigger than everyone else here. I may be sitting but I can tell as he looms over me that he must be at least 6'5" and I can see all of his muscles through his copper-colored shirt. However, they don't look like they are from working out but more from his genetics and I wonder for the first time how being part wolf can influence even those simple parts of your biology.

A weird feeling creeps into my stomach when I look up at him. It's like a sickening feeling along with burning. I almost double over in pain when someone else catches my eye in the distance.

He's beautiful. His hair runs to his ears where it curls inward. Its color, just like the others, is none I've ever seen but it's different from everyone in here including this older man. It's a deep coffee-colored base mixed in with a tangerine color that's barely noticeable that sets off his light chocolate, orange and emerald eyes. His eyes and the man before me are the only ones who differentiate from the rest of the packs. I feel my stomach give a twist and I feel myself wanting to run to this person I've never seen before. It's as if running into his arms and having them around me will make everything right.

"I see you've met everyone. Or, I should say every one of importance." He says with a smile on his face that melts me from the inside out.

Wait, I know that voice. At least I feel like I do. I look up at him again and his smile widens, "What, you don't recognize me now that I'm human?"

"Don't tease the girl." I hear Angela saying.

"Jul...Julian?" I say once the fog lifts.

He nods his head as I look from him to Angela to the man I don't know the name of as everything begins to turn black. I see everyone reach for me and hear Julian say my name. Then hot hands touch me and my body turns warm as I fall into darkness.

Chapter 11

Amberly

"I can't believe I made her faint." I hear Julian say.

I try to open my eyes but I can't seem to make my brain function right.

"What do we do now, Aaron?" I hear the alarm in Angela's voice.

"There's nothing we can do except wait for her to wake up." I hear the man named Aaron reply.

I can hear someone pacing in the distance but I'm not sure who it is.

"Well, we can't just let her sleep forever. She came here for answers and I'm sure her humans are on their way here as we speak." Julian's voice sounds very tense.

I want so much to open my eyes and run to him. I want to soothe him. Why am I feeling like this? Like I've known him for years and not days? Why are my feelings so strong for him when he's human but not when he's a wolf? How can I have this kind of connection with someone I barely know? I can feel my eyes begin to open and the light seeps through them as I squint. I look around to find three blurry forms coming to my side.

"Here let me help you. Just take it nice and slow." I hear Julian say as his hands grab my arms and my body turns to fire.

I look up at him and nearly fall off the bed as he catches me. Our faces are only centimeters apart. I can feel his even breath on my cheek as I begin to blush and look away.

Still holding me close he says, "How are you feeling?"

"I'm OK, just a little dizzy," I say as his touch leaves my skin.

I try straightening myself and I fall. I feel Julian's hands on my body as quickly as they disappear. I look at him and give a little laugh, "Guess I'm not as stable as I thought."

He smiles at me as he walks me over to the bed again, "I guess my looks are too much for you, huh?"

Before I get the chance to respond, the man they called Aaron is looking at me with confusion on his face, "Who is your mother?"

So that's his name. The older man I met before I passed out, was the man with the different eyes and blue in his hair. His name was Aaron and he must be the head of the pack or the alpha I guess because he sure knows how to get right down to business. He's the one Julian mentioned, the one who could answer all my questions.

"Why? Does that matter?"

"We were hoping it would let us know who your father might be." Angela's voice comes to me from the corner of the room where I see her sitting.

"My mother is Jocelyn Grayson but that might not be much help in finding my father because he died before I was even born, along with the rest of my family. My mother and I are the only ones left." Julian looks at me with sorrow in his eyes so I turn my gaze to the floor, not wanting to feel pitied.

A loud bang and a curse make my head jerk up. Everything happens so fast. Angela runs over to Aaron as he sinks to the ground with a bloody hand as Julian pulls me out of the room.

"Is he OK?" I look up into Julian's hard eyes and back over my shoulder in the direction of Angela and their pack leader.

"We need to talk." Is all he says as he pulls me out of the cave and into the forest again.

"OK," I answer back a little confused.

"You don't understand," Julian says as he sets me down on a rock and starts pacing.

"Understand what?"

"That man in there..."

"Aaron?" I can hear the confusion in my voice as I speak.

"Yes, Aaron."

"What about him?"

He shoots me a stomach-wrenching smile. "Wow, you are dense, aren't you? First, my looks, and now this? I think you need to see a doctor."

"Nothing's wrong with me," I say both a little bewildered and annoyed.

He looks at me out of the corner of his eye like he's baiting me, saying "Really, you're fine? Because I'm pretty sure you just fainted because of my hot looks."

Julian's quiet for a moment and I feel like I can see the wheels in his head spinning, wondering what to say next. What's the right thing and what's the wrong thing?

"You need to know." He says in a whisper as he raises his hand to his eyes and rests his elbow on the tree closest to him.

I stand up and walk over to him. I remove his hand and look into his eyes. There I see the sorrow of a thousand years.

"What do I need to know?"

"I don't know if I should be the one to tell you."

"Please." I can hear the pleading in my voice and I'm almost disgusted. "Aaron…he's your father."

Chapter 12

A aron

"It's impossible."

I'm barely aware of Angela sitting next to me on the floor. I don't understand. This isn't possible. My baby and the love of my life were lost to me all those years ago. I remember it like it was yesterday. Jocelyn passed out in my arms, hearing her family yelling for her in the distance.

"Aaron?" Angela's worried voice pulls me back from the brink of destruction.

"I'm sorry, I shouldn't have reacted that way. Please, forgive me."

She smiles at me, "There is nothing to forgive, anyone in their right mind would have acted that way. I know I would have."

"Where is she? Where is my," I pause but only for a moment before I choose to end my sentence with, "Where is Amberly?"

Angela's smile fades, "Julian, took her out of the room right after you fell to the floor."

I stand up quickly, "Is she OK?"

Angela follows suit, "Yes, she's fine. Julian did the right thing, sir."

I look down at Angela for the first time, "Yes. Yes, he did."

So many thoughts are plaguing my mind right now that I can't focus on one particular thing. My daughter is here and alive but how can that even be possible? I relive that night, every night, and I know what I heard, and what I saw. Jocelyn was not breathing, she was covered in blood, and when I listened harder I heard no heartbeat, not hers nor our daughters yet here she is. I would play it, over and over in my mind, what it would have been like if that night had played out differently, or if they had been alive. Watching my daughter grow up in front of my eyes and teaching her all about her history, her wolf history. That's when I realized for the first time that she is part of me, part wolf and I wonder if she has shifted yet. How hard life must have been for her. She didn't just grow up in a village that was meant to fear our kind but she grew up never knowing the whole truth of who she really was. Another thought enters my mind as I realize she is the only one of her kind. Half wolf and half witch and this is new territory for me, for all of us and there are so many things about her that are unknown. I just pray I know how to help her and that it's not too late.

Things are going to change now but the most important thing is she's alive and she's here and I need to teach her how to use her powers and how to control them and soon.

"Angela?"

She stands and looks at me hard, "Yes?"

"How old is my daughter now? It's felt like an eternity for me so I can't remember how many years it's been."

"I believe she is about to turn eighteen."

"Then we don't have much time."

Angela looks at me surprised before she says, "You don't think her mother would have taught her as she was growing up?"

"Sadly, I didn't have the time to explain to her mother the importance of teaching the children as they grow. She knew a lot about our kind but we never touched the subject of children, not till that night," I pause for a moment remembering when I first heard our daughter's heartbeat when I first realized I was going to be a father, "and sadly shortly after I realized she was pregnant everything happened."

Angela looks worried but once she notices me looking at her she smiles and says, "Well then we should get right to it."

I place my hand on her left shoulder and smile back. The one thing about Angela, even though she's still very young, she knows when it's time to jump and she's always the first one to do just that.

"Thank you because I'm going to need your help with her. I don't speak teenage girl." I say with a laugh and I can tell Angela is holding back one of her own.

A moment later Angela becomes serious again, "When I was talking with her it didn't seem as if she even knew about our kind. You don't think her mother never told her, do you?"

That thought had never even crossed my mind. Jocelyn not telling our daughter about me or about where she comes from. The truth is, there is no way to know what happened after that night. There is no way of knowing what she did or didn't tell our daughter, at least not until I talk to her myself. However, now I'm more afraid of a conversation with her. What if her mother didn't tell her about me? What would that mean?

"I'm sorry I didn't mean anything by it I just meant that she seemed a little surprised that she was able to communicate with Julian and if that surprised her then maybe she doesn't know but maybe I'm wrong."

The wheels start to turn in my head as Angela's words form and I realize that Jocelyn never did tell her about me and now I wonder what lies she did tell our daughter. I know they would have been to protect her but by lying and trying to protect our daughter she's done more harm than good.

"Sadly, I think you're right and we need to find her now."

Chapter 13

Amberly

"My father? Is this some kind of sick joke? My father's dead." I say as I turn away from Julian and I try to get control of the anger now bubbling in my stomach.

"According to who, you? I hope not because so far your track record is pretty spotty." I shoot him a pissed-off look and he continues. "Sorry, but it's the truth," He says with a smile.

"My mother told me he was dead."

"And Aaron thought you and your mother were dead but you're not so maybe she thought the same thing and if so then technically she didn't lie to you."

I sigh before I continue. "What did he say he thought happened to us?"

Julian looks away from me, "He didn't say. He doesn't like to talk about it. Honestly, we didn't know he even had a child until about eight years ago. It was the first time it came up, or I should say the first time he let it slip."

"So really what you're telling me is you know nothing. All you know is he has a child out there somewhere that he's always believed to be dead." I smile as I turn away from him saying, "And now you think that child is me but have no real proof."

"What more proof do we need? You live in the same village, you're about to be eighteen and your mother's name is Jocelyn. God, you are dense."

I fold my arms over my chest before continuing, "I am not, I'm just being rational."

"All the signs point to you so I think you've either gone a little loony or you're just in denial but it's one or the other." He says while lifting his pointer finger to the right side of his head and moving it in a circular motion to show he thinks I'm crazy.

"OK, so for example if someone is a princess and there is a prince under a sleeping curse the princess is expected to kiss the prince and wake him up?"

He looks at me like I've lost it, "What are you talking about?"

"Just go with me on this. If I was a princess and there was a prince who was under a sleeping spell, what would you expect me to do?" I say with my hands on my hips.

"Well first off the man would be the one to wake the princess so you're a little ass backward there, hon."

I roll my eyes, "First, off way to be sexist, and secondly just answer the questions, please."

He looks at me and lets out a very loud sigh, "Well I guess I would expect her to do the same thing as the man would do. She would have to kiss him and wake him up."

I smile and move closer to him, "OK, then just because I am a princess doesn't mean I'm the only one and it doesn't mean I will be the one to wake him up. You see?"

I get so close that he starts to back away as he says, "What I see is that you're crazier than I thought. What does this have to do with anything?"

I throw my hands up and turn away from him while almost screaming, "For crying out loud. What I mean is just because I am from the other village and my mother has the same name doesn't mean I am his daughter. Just like the princess might not be the one to wake up the prince. Man and you say I'm dense."

Julian smiles and walks over to me until we are only an inch apart. "So you're telling me you don't believe it even just a little bit? And that you feel nothing?"

I know my cheeks are turning red because I can feel the heat gathering there. I try to look away but his hand grabs my chin and forces me to look up at him again as he says. "Well?"

"I'm not saying I don't want to believe it." He looks at me confused so I continue, "I've always wanted my dad around and I've often thought about what it would have been like and how different my life would have been if he was still alive." I pause but only for a second, "But if I let myself believe this for even a moment and it's not real and you're wrong then I'm right back where I started but the pain will be ten times worse than it's ever been."

For the first time, I see something shift in his eyes almost like he wants it to be real more than I do. A moment later his hand lets go of my chin and goes around my waist and he pulls me in closer as he says, "Do you feel anything?"

I feel my cheeks get warmer and I want nothing more than to be away from him right now as I say, "I don't see what that would have to do with anything."

"Well, it's rather simple. If you're even part wolf you can feel the difference in the touch of one of our kind compared to say, a human or even someone from your village. You can also sense and smell the difference in our blood," I swear I hear him swallow and the look on his face is making me as nervous as I can feel he is. Then he says, "Everything feels different."

In the sternest voice I can muster up I say, "Let me go."

By the sadistic smile that creeps onto his face, I can tell he takes the tone of my voice as a game or maybe a challenge. His arms go tight around my back as I try to free myself. He leans down to my ear and whispers almost playfully, "Make me."

He's so close I can feel the heat of his skin on mine and his breath on my neck and ear. It sends chills up and down my spine. Eventually, I give up and stand there limp in his arms as I feel his breath move from my neck to my cheek. I look him in the eyes as he comes to face me again. Except something feels different, there's a shine in his eyes that I haven't seen before and I can tell whatever game he was playing before is over. His hands are soft against my back now and I can sense this yearning in him as it pushes itself onto me.

The way I'm feeling right now, here with him, is like nothing I've ever felt before. Everything makes sense when I'm around him and even with all the craziness going on in my life right now I feel grounded. I don't understand how I can feel this way when I've only known him a few days. Well, technically I've only known him less than an hour because until now I've only been around his wolf side. The feelings I have towards Logan took years for me to grow so how is it possible for me to feel this way about someone I barely know? Everything in my body at this moment in time is telling me to run away with him and not look back. I want to feel my lips on his and his hands on me every day.

His facial expression changes almost like he can tell what I'm thinking. I go back to our conversation in the woods when he was a wolf and I ask if the telepathy thing was only when one or both of us were in wolf form. He said it was but now looking at him I'm not so sure that's true. I can feel the heat flooding to my cheeks as the thought of him knowing what I was just thinking makes my whole body shiver. I try to turn away from him but he grips my chin lightly and looks me in the eyes as he starts to lean in closer to me. He moves very slowly almost like he's giving me a chance to pull away. A part of me wants to but everything else is screaming at him to move faster.

We are less than ten centimeters apart when we hear Angela's voice, "What in the world do you think you're doing?"

Before I can ask what's wrong Julian removes his hands from my body and walks over to stand next to Angela. I have to stop myself from reaching out for him, the absence of his hands almost hurts and the way I'm feeling is hard to explain but it's definitely something that I want to go away. I look over at Julian who is looking at Angela and I feel like I'm about to fall to pieces. I have to cross my arms around my midsection and almost hug myself to keep me from freaking out and the best part is that none of this makes sense.

Julian takes a step in the direction of the cave and my heart sinks as Angela looks at me looking at him and that's when I realize she's been talking to me.

"Are you coming?"

I answer her almost unwillingly, "Right behind you."

Chapter 14

Aaron

 Angela enters the cave first and in a split second her eyes meet mine and I know something isn't right. Before I can ask her what's wrong my daughter re-enters the cave followed shortly by Julian. I can see the redness in her cheeks and I know something happened and that's when I turn my gaze to Julian but he isn't looking at me, he's looking at my daughter. Not just looking at her but really looking. Like I used to look at her mom and suddenly I'm infuriated. I know I need to keep myself calm, as hard as that may be right now but I know it won't help matters if I freak out. My daughter doesn't even know me and the last thing I'm sure a teenage girl wants is her father putting his two cents in when it comes to her love life. Even if it is against our rules.

I take a moment to collect my thoughts and make my tone as neutral as I can when I ask, "Where were you two?"

Amberly looks in my direction hard and not with the same face she was wearing when she walked in, confused, ashamed, happy, but with one that looks pissed. *Well so much for not making her mad at me.*

"That's none of your business."

Angela turns to her but before she can talk I say, "If you are in my cave then it is my business."

"Fine then I'll leave."

Those words hit me hard, harder than I thought was possible and before I have time to form my rebuttal she is running back out the entrance as Angela and Julian go to run after her.

"No, let her go. She can't get far, she just needs some space. Today has been a long one for all of us. Julian, go to keep an eye on her, make sure she doesn't run into any trouble but keep your distance. It's getting dark so don't be long. Give her a few minutes on her own and then collect her and bring her back to the cave for the night."

Julian nods his head and then he too disappears through the cave opening.

Angela looks at me with a confused expression all over her face, "Why did you send him? And why did you let her go?"

"Because she trusts him, she knows him. At least better than she knows anyone else in this cave. So if anyone can talk to her when she's like this it's him." I turned my attention to Angela for the first time, "I let her go because from everything I remember about her mother when things were too overwhelming, as much as she wanted me there to hold her she first needed her space. Time to calm herself before she could talk about what was bothering her. So if she's anything like Jocelyn then I'm hoping when she comes back she will be more open to talking with me." I turn my attention back to the cave entrance, "Plus, she's a teenager and everything she knew about her life for the last seventeen years was just shattered in more ways than she even knows, so a few more minutes couldn't hurt, right?"

I can see Angela crossing her arms over her chest out of the corner of my eye before she replies, "Wow, when did you become all-knowing ?"

I look down to see her smiling at me.

"It was a guess."

She sounds impressed when she says, "Well it was a good one. Guess you've got this teenager thing down."

I turn my attention back to the cave entrance as I say, "Not fast enough apparently."

Angela drops her arms and her smile vanishes as she replies, "She doesn't understand yet but soon she will just give it some time. Like you said, it's been a long day for all of us."

"Well until that time comes, I stick by my earlier statement. I'm going to need your help with her."

She flashes a smile that shows all her teeth, "I'm not going anywhere. Like I could leave you to fend for yourself."

We look at one another as we burst out in laughter together both thinking the same thing I'm sure.

Chapter 15

A

mberly

Of all the nerve. He thinks he's my father for what an hour, so that gives him the right to tell me what to do, well no sir. I look around the empty forest hoping I can figure out which way home is. We came so far and Julian was so fast that I don't remember which way is which.

Lost in my thoughts I almost don't notice the growling and branches breaking behind me. I don't need to turn around to know it's a wolf and not one of the friendly kind. I take off at a sprint through the woods and I can feel the breath of the wolf on my legs. I'm running as fast as my body will let me but I can tell it's not making much difference and the wolf is gaining. I feel almost stupid because there is no way I'm outrunning a wolf, right now he's just playing with me, enjoying the chase. I know wolves normally hunt in packs so I just hope it's only one because my chances of getting out of this are already slim. I haven't been practicing on my spells enough to really make much of a difference, at least not up against a wolf. Plus, with each spell I use I get weaker and weaker so I would probably pass out, and then the wolf would have me for dinner. Then of course there are like a million and one rules I would be breaking if I did use my powers.

Feeling hopeless, knowing there's no way I'm making it out of this one, I start to slow but then my body begins to ache all over and somehow I begin to run faster. I've never run this fast in my life, I can barely tell where one leg starts and the other ends and I know a human can't run this fast. The pendant around my neck begins to get hot and as the seconds drag on it gets hotter and hotter until it's too much. It feels like it's starting to burn my skin where it lays against my bare chest. If it wasn't bouncing all over the place from me running so fast I think I would have a third-degree burn on my chest. I want to rip it off my neck but I need to focus on running.

I can tell I put some distance between us but not much. Suddenly a sharp pain works its way through my body. It starts at my stomach and spreads through my sides. It gets stronger and stronger until it's too much and my foot gets caught up under my other and I go flying. The wind gets knocked out of me, as I try to gasp for air I turn around to see the wolf is only five feet away and ready to close the distance with one more leap. I close my eyes anticipating the attack with no time to react. Then my body gets heavy and I feel a surge of energy like never before. My body jolts forward as all my energy is drained from my body and I fall back to the earth floor. I hear a yelp then some whimpering. It's hard to open my eyes but when I finally do I see the wolf about fifteen feet from where my body now lays on the ground. It's trying to stand but its efforts only make it wobble more. It lies there for a few moments before it tries again. I take that time to try to stand but I have nothing left and that's when I realize the heat of the necklace is no longer there. It's now cold against my skin. I enclose it in the palm of my hand as my eyes close and my head falls to the ground. All my strength, all my fight is gone.

In seconds the amulet starts to get hot again as it burns the skin of my hand. I almost let it fall back to my chest but I don't even have the energy to release it. I hear the breaking of branches as the wolf gets closer, seconds later a new kind of pain engulfs the right side of my body as I feel its sharp teeth sink into my skin. It continues to bite and claw at my arms and stomach. I'm trying to think about anything other than the pain as I suppress the need to scream out. I can feel the heat of its breath all over me, practically engulfing me and that's when I notice it for the first time. It's hot and sticky as it makes its way down my body and to the dirt-covered earth.

My blood.

I try to kick the wolf off but I can't lift my legs so instead I try to punch at him with my free arm but it doesn't even faze him. I know I'm too weak to use my powers; I can barely focus or get up the energy to keep my eyes open. I can feel the world caving in on me as my sight starts to fade. Before everything turns pitch black I can make out a human silhouette on the hill.

Julian.

"Noooo!" I hear him shout as he pulls off his shirt and from here I see what looks like the same birthmark I have but his is on his lower stomach and when I say the same I mean down to the number of circles behind the raven. I try to focus on it but the pain is too much and I can feel my blood running down my body. I know I'm going to pass out soon but I don't want to take my eyes off him. I know I should be fighting back but I don't have the strength. I look into Julian's eyes and I see hatred and determination like I've never seen before. He looks at me for only a second as our eyes meet, and then I feel myself slipping as he looks away from me and turns his attention to the wolf as he jumps through the air and shifts in mid-air.

Then everything goes black.

Chapter 16

Aaron

"Where are they? It's getting dark."

I guess Angela knows me better than I would care to admit because in the next moment, she's putting her hand on my shoulder, a gesture to try to calm me but it's not helping much. I thought I kept my voice level and didn't show how concerned I really was but apparently I didn't since she noticed.

It's hard to believe that it was eleven years ago that I brought her back to our cave. She has grown into such a strong woman and I'm glad to have her as one of my Beta's but also my packs Mu. She has always helped to keep the peace among everyone in the pack and be there to calm any situation, like my current one. My father, our last alpha, had told me to never bring an outsider into the pack. It was one of those so-called rules but I'm glad that I'm a rule breaker because look at her now. She's also not the only one in my pack who is an outsider, most here are from other packs but I think we are better as a whole because of it.

"I need to go and find her," I say as I begin to stand.

Angela follows my lead, "You sent Julian out with her, she'll be fine."

"You don't know-"

Before I can finish I fall over in pain. I feel like my body is being ripped apart. Like teeth and nails are separating my flesh. I can see Angela's lips moving frantically but I hear nothing. Next thing I know I have a room full of worried faces and strong hands trying to get me to a bed.

It's more than the feeling of the nails and teeth. I'm also getting glimpses. It's like a puzzle and I can only see fragments. Despite how little I do see I know it's Julian and panic takes over the pain as I stand upright waving everyone off with a hand, "I'm fine. But... something's wrong." I push past them and head to the cave entrance. I don't know how long I was on the floor for but I know it was long enough when I looked into the forest and see Julian holding Amberly limp in his arms.

* * *

Julian

I look down at her blood-covered face and the need to walk faster engulfs me but for some reason, my legs won't carry me any further. I drop to the ground but I hold her tightly so she never comes close to touching the dirt. I lift a hand to move her blood-covered hair out of her face and I notice right away how pale she looks.

"You'll be OK. I promise you'll be OK."

I don't understand why she hasn't started to heal. Her heart never stopped, it only slowed so there's no reason she shouldn't have started to heal by now. I know she has our blood running in her veins so she should have our fast healing as well. I just pray her witch side isn't getting in the way because if she doesn't start to heal herself soon I don't think she will make it through the night.

This is all my fault. If I had only been closer, and ran faster this wouldn't have happened. I start to stand again and almost fall and I would have if it weren't for the strong hands that are now covering my body. I'm so out of it that I didn't notice any of my pack around me till this moment. *How long have they been here?*

"Julian, what happened, is she ok?" Angela's voice pulls me from my thoughts and I look up to see her coming my way and Aaron not far behind.

I sigh and look at the ground. "One minute I was following her and the next she was running. It took me a moment, too long of one, to realize she was running from a wolf. I didn't get there in time."

Aaron pushes his way past the rest of the pack until he is standing in front of me. He bends over so he can grab Amberly out of my arms and then he turns and walks away with her. "You did fine. I'll take her now." And that's when it sinks in. I realize how much I failed not just myself but him. He may be saying I did fine but really he is angry with me and he should be. He stops walking for a moment to look back at me and then the rest of our pack before he continues, "Everyone make sure he gets the help he needs. Those cuts look bad."

I look at Angela, "I'm fine."

"No, you're not." She pauses to look me over before adding, "Are you telling me you don't feel anything right now?" She continues to look at me as she gestures to the others to help.

I look down at myself for the first time and now I see what they are talking about. When I was in the fight with the wolf I didn't feel the blows it was returning. But now I can see there were many because my body is covered in blood. Some mine and some Amberly's. I look back at Angela, "Really, I'm fine I just want to make sure she's OK."

I start to walk away and Angela gently grabs my arm, "She'll be fine. If anyone can save her it's her father. But for now, we need to worry about you."

Knowing she's not going to stop till I give in I take a step towards the entrance and my legs give out. I feel strong hands under my arms and on my back and then the darkness surrounds me. I see Amberly's face as I close my eyes and surrender to the darkness.

Chapter 17

Jocelyn

It's already been four long days since the boys left to go find my daughter and with each passing second, I can feel myself going a little more crazy. I don't know how we got to this place. I've tried so hard to protect her and keep the truth from her so she wouldn't feel the hurt that I've been carrying all these years. After all, isn't it a mother's job to protect their child from the world and all the hurt it can hold?

I have seen over the years the void that has grown in her heart because of the absence of her father and I felt that was a secret I needed to take to my grave, along with all the other ones from that night eighteen years ago. However, now I'm wondering if I should have chosen a different path. If I had told her the truth would we be closer? Would she have still left the village? There's no real way to know and the only thing I do know is I need to fix mine and my daughters relationship and soon before there's nothing left to save.

When the boys bring her home I'm going to tell her everything, as hard as it's going to be and as angry as she's going to be it has to be done if we are going to move forward. I just wish I could change this life for her. I wish I could bring back her father and not just for my sake. I just want so much more for her than what I've had. That's why all the lies and that's why I don't want her learning to use her magic because I've seen all the hurt and destruction it can bring and most of all I've seen how it can change a person. I've changed and not for the better because of mine. I've done things I wish I could take back, things that will tear apart our village from the inside. Sometimes I wish I could get rid of my magic and give away my title as the leader of this village and just leave and start fresh with Amberly but I know that's not possible. Then when I think about how she will have to take over after I'm gone only makes me want to fight to stay around as long as possible to spare her from this. It's not an easy life, people crave power but what they don't know is what happens, how you feel when you have it, and the things you can lose because of it.

It's hard being responsible for everyone and the fear of making one wrong decision, like I did with my daughter. You can be responsible for the end of everything when you are in charge and if you're not careful the power can corrupt even the best of people.

The only thing I care about right now is getting my daughter back home safe and telling her the truth about that night. It's going to change her life and not for the better but it needs to be done. I just pray I haven't made this decision too little too late.

Chapter 18

Troy

I've known Logan since the day I was born so it's safe to say I know everything about the guy and I've seen him in every mood possible but this one I've never seen before. It's been four long days since we left home and came into this dark and damp forest in search of Amberly but not once has he stopped. I've had to even force him to sleep for a few hours here and there. He's like a dog in search of its bone.

I knew it long before he did, the way he feels for Amberly. His feelings grew slowly but I feel that only made them stronger. He already cared for her like I do but now it's on another level and part of me wonders what it must feel like. Not to just be in love or even that strongly in love but to have that person you feel that strongly for be so far out of your reach and not know where they are or if they are even still alive. Part of me wonders how he's keeping himself together at all right now.

"Hey, man it's getting pretty late, maybe we should call it for the night."

Logan looks up to the sky for the first time in hours and it's like he's just now realizing it's dark out as he says, "It's been four days, Troy. If we don't catch up to her soon I don't know if we ever will."

"Man, listen you're the best tracker in the village and so far you've had no problem knowing which way to go so I'm sure a few hours from now the trail will be the same." I pause but only for a moment to look at him. I can see the dark circles under his eyes and his hands are starting to shake slightly and I know he's sleep-deprived. "Just for a few hours man. You'll be of no use to her if you don't get some rest and you know that as well as I do."

Logan closes his eyes for the first time and keeps them closed as his hand finds a home over them and he lets out a sigh as he says, "Fine, but as soon as the sun is in the sky we keep going."

"Deal."

Logan slides to the ground a moment later and I can see what a toll this trip is taking on him. I hope we find Amberly fast because I don't know how much longer he can push himself like this. I'm sure, just like me, he is wondering why she is traveling so far away from home but that's something I know better than to talk about, at least right now. Amberly has always told Logan everything that goes on with her but this time something was different. Whatever is going on with her is bigger than anything she's ever dealt with before in her life and the fact that she wouldn't share it with us, especially with him, only makes me worry more about what we are walking into. It doesn't feel like she wants to be found, not with how much distance she has put between her and her home. Everything she's ever known she walked away from and that for me is the biggest thing because one thing

Amberly doesn't like is change or starting something new but yes here we are.

For the first time, I caught myself wondering what she could be doing or thinking about right now. I mean she's always been very rational and smart so for her to do something this dramatic has me wondering what could have changed so fast. She said it had nothing to do with being afraid when she encountered the wolf and that much I believe because she never would have come back out here on her own if that's what she was afraid of. No, there's something deeper going on but what?

I look back over to where Logan is now lightly snoring and I smile. I'm happy he finally passed out because he needed it the most. I look up into the night sky, close my eyes as I think of Amberly, and moments later sleep finds me.

Chapter 19

L ogan

I wake up to the sound of Troy snoring and I have to fight back the urge to hit him. I'm about to roll over until I notice it's almost light out. Every bone in my body hurts and I would love to continue lying here and getting more rest but I know we need to get moving. I try to stand but fall back to the ground as a sharp pain shoots up my leg. It's asleep.

I slap my leg around a little to try to wake it up as I think about Amberly. I can't ever remember a day passing without us being around each other at some point, so the last four days have not only been weird but they've been the hardest of my life. I've gotten so used to having her around that I never thought the day would come when I'd go through the day without her, let alone four days.

Somewhere over our years together my feelings for her changed, grew. I don't see her the same way anymore and sometimes I wish I could go back but I'm way past that now. Over the course of this trip, I've thought a lot about what I would say when I saw her and I think I've made up my mind. I'm scared of how our relationship is going to change but I need to tell her how I feel. I've never been so afraid of anything in my life, the thought of losing her or Troy is hard for me to think about. I've been with them both every day of my life and they have become a part of who I am today so the thought of her turning her back on me or our relationship not being the same after I tell her scares me.

Troy draws my attention back to him as he starts to stir in his sleep. I test my leg again, it's awake. I make my way over to where he is still sleeping and I can't help smiling at him as I lift my leg and kick him in the side ever so lightly. He practically jumps up off the ground and throws his hands up like he's ready for a fight and I have to stifle a laugh.

His eyes adjust and he looks at me as he lowers his hands and says, "What's up?"

"It's almost light, it's time to get moving."

I turn away from Troy as he sighs before saying, "Man, you said sunlight not before. You're killing me, man."

Without turning around to look at him I say, "Just get up. You're not going to be able to get back to sleep and you know it so mine as well get the day started."

"All I have to say is you're lucky you're like a brother to me because if not man your ass would be mine right now."

I turn to look at him as the smile on my face gets bigger and I raise my hand and gesture for him to come to me, "Let's go then. Take a shot."

That gets Troy up, in the next moment I'm bracing myself for his attack as he runs towards me. I figure a few-minute delay won't hurt.

Chapter 20

Julian

My mind is racing a mile a minute. I can't get her blood-covered face out of my mind. Knowing it's my fault, I should have been closer. Everyone keeps telling me I did a good job and it could have been worse. All they have to do is look at my face to know I'm beating myself up for what happened. I haven't said one word to anyone. It's like I can't speak. What if she's not OK?

The door opens and I almost jump off the bed, if it wasn't for the hands of my pack all over me keeping me on the bed I would have. Angela walks in and I relax again. She gestures for the others to leave the room and I wonder if that's her way of getting them out to tell me the bad news because right now I can't read her facial expression like I normally can.

I reach up and grab her right hand once she's close enough to do so. Everyone is on edge right now, I can practically feel John and Dean's nails come out on my skin to keep me in place like they are afraid of what I'll do next. Dean and John aren't much older than Angela and I but they are stronger, for the moment, then I am. I relax a little because the last thing I need to do is start a fight with them, Aaron would have my head.

Angela places her free hand on Dean's broad shoulder in a way to relax him. However, I find myself questioning how she could reach his shoulders with how tall he is. Dean removes his hands from my body and looks at John to do the same. Angela starts to remove her hand from Dean and I wonder if her hand will get caught in his long raven hair. It's always pulled back in a ponytail but right now it's hanging loosely around his shoulders.

Looking at John, Angela says, "You can both go now. I need to look over his wounds."

John's voice is hoarse when he replies, "Are you sure Angela? What if you need us to hold him down because of the pain?"

Angela looks at me then and I know she can see it in my eyes. I'm not feeling that kind of pain right now.

"I think I've got it covered but thank you, John."

Dean comes around the other side of the bed to put his hands on John's less broad shoulders and at the same moment his head gestures for the door. Defeated John sighs and looks at Angela as he says, "Ok, but call if you need us. We will be right outside the door."

Angela nods her head in agreement as they exit the room and she lets out a long-suppressed sigh and I can't help but look at her funny.

"What's wrong? Is she OK?"

Angela looks at me for what seems to be the first time as she starts to lift up my mangled shirt to expose my even more mangled skin. She winces when she gets a good look and I grab her hand again to draw her attention back to my face.

"Angela, is she OK?"

"I don't know. Aaron is with her. He won't let anyone else in the room right now."

Panic spreads through my body as I sit up and close my eyes from the pain. Angela's hands are firm on my shoulders when she says, "You need to rest and I need to look you over. Once I'm done here I will go and insist that he lets me in. But first I need to look at you."

"No, you need to look at her first."

"He won't let anyone in right now, Julian. So the faster I get done looking you over I can go and tell him I'm done with you and then I can help her."

I can feel the anger starting to take control and I know she can see it lingering in my eyes when I turn all my attention to her and say, "Lie. Tell him you already looked me over."

"You know I can't do that."

"I need you to." I pause, afraid to speak, afraid she will see what's hidden under the words. "I need to know she's OK."

I can see the understanding in her eyes when she replies, "I know you do and I promise as soon as I look at her you will be the first to know," she pauses and looks back at my body, "But first we need to get you patched up."

Angela lifts my shirt again to expose my blood-covered abdomen and I can see worry in her eyes now. Her eyes catch mine as she says, "Julian, you need to allow yourself to heal."

I look away from her before I say, "I don't want to," I pause for only a second and then I look back into her eyes to make sure she can see all the secrets that lie inside, "Not until I'm sure she's OK."

Angela smiles, "You always were stubborn and I'm pretty sure I've mentioned a few times that that would be your undoing."

I can't help but laugh and wince at the same time when I reply, "Yes, yes you have and it seems you were right."

I feel defeated when I fall back to the bed and my head hits the pillow. I feel fatigued and I want to get up but my body won't let me. That's when I see the needle in my leg as Angela pulls it back from my skin and mouths an

'I'm sorry' as everything goes dark.

* * *

Julian

I wake up hours later but this time I feel the pain and the stiffness that goes along with it. I lift my shirt one more time to see my wounds are almost completely healed and I can't help but be annoyed at Angela.

Sitting up takes some doing and it's hard to believe I can feel this stiff in a few short hours. My attention goes to the door when Angela walks back through it. A smile plastered along her face makes me sit up straight but when her eyes find me across the room her smile falters but only a little and I brace myself.

"Hey, you how are we feeling?"

I cross my arms over my chest and stare at her.

"Not mad at me I hope. I had to do it, you were being too stubborn and you wouldn't let me help and you wouldn't heal yourself, so I had no choice."

Frustration clear on my face Angela puts her hands up in surrender. "Look I had to do what I had to do."

"How is she?"

"Listen I get it, I do but you need to focus on you right now. You're of no use to anyone if you don't take the time to-"

Getting more than a little annoyed I cut her off as I try not to let it show in my voice when I say, "Angela! I don't care. Now tell me."

I hear her let out a sigh before she says, "Listen, she's not, not ok but she's not doing any better either."

In the next moment, my feet are hitting the floor and a sharp pain jolts up my legs but I ignore it as I make my way to the door with Angela on my heels saying my name over and over again. I get to the room they have her in, it's hard to explain how I know this is the right room but I just know and it's verified when I reach for the doors and Angela jumps in front of me.

"Listen, he needs time with her. He's trying to help her and by going in there it's only going to distract him and take time away from trying to help her."

Knowing she's right I drop my hands to my sides. "I can't just sit here and do nothing."

"You're not. You're going to come with me and we are going to talk."

"Talk. Seriously?"

Angela wraps her left arm through my right one and tugs me lightly away from the doors. "Yes, seriously."

We make our way out of the cave entrance and find a nice place to sit. I'm not sure what she wants from me but I know without a doubt she's waiting for me to talk first as she sits and stares at me. It feels like she's waiting for me to snap like everyone is. They are so used to that side of me I guess I can understand but since she's been here things have been different with me.

"Can you stop looking at me like that please?"

She looks almost surprised when she responds, "Like what?"

"Like you're waiting for me to snap."

"Look I'm sorry but can you blame me?"

I look at the ground before answering. "No. I get it but I'm not the same person I was."

Angela lets out a loud obnoxious scoff before she says, "What's that supposed to mean? Do you not recall not even a week ago when you almost took out John's eye for just looking at you the wrong way?"

I have to suppress a laugh when I answer. "Hey, he was looking at me like he wanted a fight. I don't care what anyone says. So I was ready to give him one."

Now it's Angela who has to suppress a laugh but she isn't doing a very good job of it. "OK, good so you do remember."

"Yes, but I meant what I said, I'm not that same guy."

I catch Angela half rolling her eyes, kind of like she was trying to stop herself right in the middle of doing the action, "Julian, that was only a week ago."

I look deep into the forest, in the same direction as Amberly's home before I answer, "I know."

"No one can change that big of a thing about themselves in such a short time. That's who you've always been. That person is a part of you and who you are. I'm not trying to be an ass or criticize, I'm just stating a fact. I'm not saying it's not possible to change that part of you if that's what you wanted to do," she pauses for a moment to smile but only a little, "which if you want my opinion I think it's a good thing to work on a change. However, something like that will take months if not years."

I look up into the trees above to see a small opening out into the sky and I smile when I reply. "I don't know how to explain it. Everything you're saying makes sense and I know you're right. I know you can't change something that big about yourself overnight but somehow I did." I close my eyes for what feels like an eternity before I finish saying, "It's her. She's changing me."

Once the words are out I know there's no taking them back and I know that Angela will now know my secret. My forbidden secret. Sitting here I keep my eyes closed never wanting to open them again. Wanting only to feel this way and wanting only to see her face coming to me from the darkness, forever.

Chapter 21

Angela

Once I hear those words leave his mouth I have no doubt that what I've been sensing is now confirmed. Looking at him with his eyes closed I can see the peace on his face as he sits there next to me on the rocks.

"You're in love with her."

It wasn't a question, more of a statement. I had a feeling he was the moment he came home, there was just something so different about him. Then there was the way he would look at her, talk to her, or even just talk around her. Everything about him was different but not in a bad way. It's like she woke him up, brought him to life, gave him a purpose but yet the only thing I keep thinking about is how I wish he felt this way about anyone else.

"Those are your words, not mine. All I said is she's changing me. For the better."

Not wanting to say the words but knowing they need to be said, "Julian. You know it's forbidden."

He stands up so fast it takes my eyes a moment to readjust.

"I never said I loved her, you did."

"But you're not denying it either."

The realization is all over his face when he finally notices that I'm right.

"Julian, I wish it was different, I do, but you know how a pack works."

"It doesn't matter. The only thing that matters is that she's OK."

I can feel my heart breaking for him as I see the hurt clear as day in his eyes, "We will figure it out OK?"

I see the light leaving his eyes as he answers back, "There's nothing to find out."

Julian turns away from me and makes his way back to the cave entrance but I put myself between the two as I say, "I need to hear you say it."

"Say what?"

"Tell me you're not in love with her."

There's nothing but silence and I know I'm waiting for something that will never come because the one thing about Julian is he never lies and he isn't going to start now.

"If you can't tell me you don't love her then tell me you do."

Julian closes his eyes as he looks up towards the heavens and away from me as he replies in such a whisper that I need to strain to hear his words as they leave his barely parted lips, "I'm in love with her," he is quiet for what feels like an eternity before he opens his eyes and looks down at me, "There Angela you happy now?"

I can see the anger in his eyes but I know it's only to hide the sorrow that is right behind them. I reach out and put my hand on his arm but I can tell he wants to pull away and almost does until I close my fingers around his arm and make him look me in the eyes when I say, "I can see how much you care for her. I also know it's against all our laws," Julian looks away from me once more as those last few words leave my lips. I can see he wants to run. To run from all the hurt and all the things he wants and feels he can't have but before he gets the chance I continue, "However, if there is a way for you to be with her then I will help you find it." Julian looks at me for what feels like the first time and I continue as though I never stopped speaking, "I will see if I can talk to her and then talk to Aaron. Aaron listens to me, and if she feels the same way you do, we will find a way."

I can see the light slowly returning to his eyes and the hope that lies within them now. "You would do that?"

"Julian, if you don't know this by now then you don't know me at all, but there's nothing I wouldn't do for you. Just like there's nothing you wouldn't do for me. I can see she makes you happy, she makes you the best version of yourself. You're the person I always knew you could be and that's because of her. I want that all for you. So if there is a way then we will find it. Together."

A little taken aback by the look on Julian's face I'm about to ask why he still looks worried but before I can get the words out he says in a weary tone, "You know he's not going to be happy about this. Let alone want me anywhere near her once he knows, right?"

Now it's my turn to look away. I know Aaron is a strong-headed man and I know how everyone else perceives him in the pack but I know him best. I know that if Amberly tells me she feels the same way for Julian and she wants to be with him then I know without a doubt, given some time, that I can make Aaron see my side. "Like I said, just leave it to me."

"But Angela I don't want him to become cross with you all because of me. He's used to being unhappy with me but when it comes to you..."

"That's my point exactly."

Julian playfully rolls his eyes and I can see him starting to let his guard down again for the first time since our conversation started. He lets out a half fake sigh as he says, "Thanks a lot Angela, you weren't supposed to agree with me."

I shrug my shoulders, "Hey, you said it not me and who am I to disagree when the facts are true," the right side of my mouth comes up in a smile when I continue, "You're always on his bad side, whereas I'm always on his good side." I look to the night sky and tap my pointer finger on the tip of my chin. "Hey, that means I'm the good child and you're the bad one, I never really thought of it that way till now."

Julian nudges his shoulder into mine lightly in a playful manner before I continue with a smile on my face and a cocky know it all tone in my voice, "Hey, not my fault I'm his favorite."

It feels nice to see him so at peace even though I know he is still worried about how Aaron will handle this. The one thing I do know is I need to get on this soon before Julian does what he does best. Messes it up or gives up all hope.

Chapter 22

Julian

Telling Angela the truth was the hardest thing I think I've ever had to do. It's not just that I'm not really one to show my feelings but it's also because of what those feelings mean. It's hard enough to admit when you like someone in the pack but it's a whole other thing entirely when the one who you want to be with, the one who you think about 24/7 is your alpha's daughter. And to make matters worse, it's not like she's been living in our pack. Aaron didn't even know about her till a few days ago, so he hasn't even had time to get to know his daughter or to make that father-daughter bond. He just got her back; he's not going to want to let her out of his sight let alone waste a minute with her once she recovers, and she will.

Despite everything I'm glad if someone had to know how I feel, it's Angela. It's always been Angela. Since she first came here to live with us we have been like two peas in a pod. Her being the good one and me the not-so-good one. I showed her the ropes and kept everyone off her back when she got here and as we grew we learned to have each other's backs through everything, no matter what it was. Other than Aaron, we are the only ones who know all of each other's deep dark secrets. Like our birthmarks and our extra, how should I put this, our extra gifts I guess I could say. We know everything about each other.

I peer inside Amberly's room and see that for the first time no one is in there with her. I use this opportunity to go in and see her for the first time since the attack. I would be lying if I didn't admit that I was scared. Not only of someone catching me in here with her but also of seeing her and seeing how badly she's hurt.

Slowly I make my way across the pitch dark room. Human eyes wouldn't be able to put one foot in front of the other in here, if it weren't for my wolf half neither would I but it's as easy finding my way around in here as it is outside. I reach her bedside in a few short strides. Her hair and face have been cleaned and her hair has been neatly placed to the right side of her face. Her whole body seems to have been washed because I see no blood but just because I don't see it doesn't mean I can't smell it. Her arms lay limp next to her body and I can tell her fresh clothes are too small from the way they cling to her body. The bandages around her abdomen are visible at the hem of her shirt and that's when I realized why I was smelling blood. The bandages aren't white but more of a crimson color. There's barely any white left to the part that I can see and that worries me a little.

Trying to keep myself calm I take her hand in mine and bring my forehead down to meet our hands as I rest them against it. I sit like this for a long time and then I lift my head and kiss the back of her hand before placing it back to her side where I found it only minutes earlier. I stand but before turning to leave I kiss her on the forehead then I lean my forehead against hers as I say just loud enough for her to hear.

"I'm so sorry."

I close my eyes as I feel the moisture building in them, "Please, come back to me. I can't lose you, not after finally getting to be near you." I open my eyes and stand up straight to look at her. "Watching you for so long I got to know the real you, even the parts of yourself that you hid from those closest to you. I saw something in you that mirrored all the parts of me I had long since lost and you woke those parts back up. Admitting how I feel or showing my emotions has never been easy for me but with you I want to be that person. I would be lying if I didn't say I wasn't mad at myself for wasting so much time." I look over at the door before I continue, "I should have approached you sooner. You would have found your dad sooner and well I, I would have felt this sooner."

I can hear someone coming down the hall. I pause to listen harder and realize it's Aaron, I'd know his shuffle anywhere. I lean down to kiss her on the forehead once more and say, "I promise I'll never let anything happen to you again. Please, fight." I look down at her one last time before heading for the door. "I'll come back soon."

* * *

Julian

"Julian," Aaron calls to me as I pass him in the hall. I was hoping he would have kept walking.

I turn around to face him, "Yes, sir?"

I can tell he's forcing a smile as he stands there. "I wanted to thank you."

Taken aback I ask, "Thank me?"

"If it wasn't for you my daughter would have died and she never would have made it back to the cave in time."

"Sir, I didn't do anything-"

"You fought off that wolf and then you carried her all the way home even as you were bleeding out yourself. You did more than you give yourself credit for, son. You gave her a fighting chance."

As he finishes his sentence he puts his hand on my shoulder and all I can do is look at it. There is so much I want, no I need to say, but the words won't come out of my mouth. How can he be thanking me when it should have never happened? Before I can find my words he pats me on the shoulder and continues on his way to Amberly's room but not without a final word.

"And stop calling me, sir. I don't know how many times I need to tell you that, Julian." With a smile on his face, a real one this time, he walks into the room and out of site.

* * *

Angela

Aaron passes me on the way to his daughter's room but he's not what catches my attention, it's Julian standing like a statue only a few feet away. I walk over to him slowly, trying not to startle him. When I reach his side I can tell he still doesn't take notice of me so I place my hand on his which lies at his side. The moment our skin touches I see the light come back into his eyes like he's waking up for the first time.

"Julian?"

"Sorry, I must have dozed off. Think I need some sleep."

I've known Julian almost all his life so it's not that hard to tell when he's trying to be evasive. However, today is not the day I will let it go.

"Julian."

"Angela?"

"What's going on?"

"Nothing."

I can't help but let out an annoyed sigh, "Julian, please don't play me for stupid. I've known you a long time and I know when something is going on. Just like our earlier conversation."

Julian looks down at me as the lines in his face become deeper which shows me he's annoyed with me. Without a word, he turns his back to me and starts to walk away and I walk after him.

"You snuck in to see her didn't you?"

Nothing but silence.

"Julian, will you please talk to me."

He stops so fast that I almost walk into the back of him.

"What do you want me to say, Angela? Yes, I snuck in to see her. Yes, she's still not awake and yes I blame myself."

I can't help but fold my arms over my chest, "Well, it's a start."

Julian stomps off mumbling and I know I shouldn't be pushing his buttons like I normally do, not right now, but I can't help but try to go on like normal. If I don't I think everyone will go mad. But I know when it's time to leave Julian be and right now is the time. With one final look in the direction he disappeared in I pushed open the door to Amberly's room and saw Aaron sitting by her side and even from this distance I can see the pain all over his face. As one tear escapes his eye I make my way into the room and silently close the door behind me.

Chapter 23

Logan

It feels like we've been walking for months instead of days. At this point, I feel like we are never going to find her. Just as I'm about to give up all hope something catches my eye. I look down and find a small piece of cloth covered in blood and right away I know it's from Amberly's clothes because it's part of the outfit she wore when she left the village. I try not to let the panic take over but I fail miserably.

My head shoots up with the cloth still in my hand. I look around the woods, "Amberly!" I scream her name over and over each time a little louder.

I can't hear anything, only a ringing inside my head as my vision starts to blur. It takes me a while to realize Troy is in front of my face with his hands on my shoulders shaking me and screaming my name over me screaming hers. For the first time, he sees the cloth in my hand and I can see the realization on his face as he turns around himself and starts to yell her name with me.

* * *

Troy

It's been hours since Logan found the cloth with Amberly's blood on it but yet somehow I know we are getting closer. I've always tried to be the weird, funny one but right now it's like I'm someone completely different.

I've always messed with Amberly, hard. Never once let up on her, always cracking jokes. She's always been like a little sister to me and it's just now starting to set in that she's out here somewhere all alone and hurt and I could have prevented that. If I had only held onto her a little tighter for a little longer she never would have gotten out of the gate in the first place.

The thought of never seeing her smile again or hearing her contagious laugh brings an ache to my chest that I've never experienced before. Amberly has always been the best of our group, she's what brought us and kept us together this long. She's our sanity and our voice of reason. We have to find her.

For the first time, I can feel it in my gut, like nothing I've ever felt before, we are going to find her. With that, I get the push I need as I grab Logan by the shirt and start to run deeper into the forest.

Chapter 24

Angela

Sitting next to Aaron I'm unsure for the first time of what I should do. What should I say? Should I say anything? He's been sitting here almost a full day, which makes this day four since the attack. I've sat here with him almost the whole time, only leaving to make sure everything is OK with the rest of the pack and Julian and to get Aaron something to drink and eat, which he refuses.

Julian hasn't been seen or heard from since I last saw him in the hall. It's hard to believe one girl can change our world so much and in such a short time. Her presence has changed everyone in some way, shape, or form. Some, like Aaron, Julian, and myself, more than others. We've barely had any time to really get to know her but at the same time, it's like she's always been here with us like we've always known her. So it doesn't feel weird to me that Aaron, someone I've never once seen shed a tear, cries at her bedside or that Julian has already fallen in love with her. The main reason why I understand is because I feel it. She feels like a long-lost best friend or better yet a sister to me. I feel the absence of her all around me.

It's hard to understand but it's clear as day and I find myself for the first time thinking how different our world will be if she doesn't wake up. The impact on our lives would be catastrophic at her loss. Just like having her around has changed us all for the better it would do just the opposite if we lost her.

* * *

Julian

Making my way into the cave I feel a little lighter than I have all day. It's like the closer I get to her the less I feel weighed down. When I enter the cave everyone is trying to talk to me but I keep walking, with only one destination in mind. I reach the doors and hesitate, but only for a moment before I push them open as quietly as I can.

I see Aaron and Angela sitting beside Amberly's bed but only Angela turns her head in my direction. Aaron, holding his daughter's hand, seems like he's in a trance. Beforc I can say a word Angela gets up and makes her way over to me by the door. She smiles as she places her hand on my arm and without a second thought I smile back.

Angela and I have been so close for so long it's like we can communicate to each other with one look. To many people that can be a scary thought but for me it's comforting to know someone so well that you can calm them with only a look or a touch. My heart skips a beat when I see how still Amberly still is. Without a second thought, I close my eyes and let out a quiet sigh.

Chapter 25

Amberly

The pain is unbearable but I don't make a sound. If I had to describe to someone the pain I'm feeling I would say it feels like my blood is boiling under my skin. I want to focus on something, anything else but I'm finding it very hard because every time I do the pain seems to increase. It makes its way from my chest to my fingertips and then to my stomach where it seems to take up residence. After some time the pain becomes less and I take this time to focus on my surroundings.

I feel someone holding my hand but it's not familiar to me. I try to open my eyes to see who it is but they feel like they are glued shut. I try harder but they barely open, only enough to see a few shadows as they start to sting so I give up. I try to remember what happened and where I am but everything is foggy. Then I hear their voices and everything starts flooding back. It doesn't take me long to remember Julian and the forest and my dead father coming back to life. All the memories of the last few days are coming at me so fast that I feel a headache forming. Then my last memory floods my mind. The wolf. The thought makes me wince as I remember the feeling of its teeth on my skin, as I remember the pain.

Then I hear his voice, Julian, "Aaron, how is she?"

I can hear Aaron sigh before he answers, "She's still very weak." I can hear the concern in his voice and all I want to do is tell them I'm fine but the words won't form. "I'm hoping that the wolf blood running in her veins will help her start to heal soon. If it doesn't…"

Julian's reply sounds strained, "What will happen if her blood, our blood doesn't start to heal her?"

I realize now it was Aaron who was holding my hand because he gently lays it next to me and then I hear him walk over to where I believe Julian and Angela are standing, "She's been suppressing that side of who she is. I don't think her mother ever told her about her wolf side because she hasn't been showing any signs of her wolf blood and because of that she is denying that part of her. Unless she comes to terms with it, it won't help her."

I hear Julian sigh, "I get that, what I'm asking is what will happen if she doesn't?"

Aaron pauses for a long while but when he finally answers he says the words so fast that I barely catch them, "I'm afraid she won't make it."

A loud bang sounds in my ears as it reaches me from across the room and I try harder this time to open my eyes and slowly they give in. I look over in the direction I heard the bang come from and it takes a few moments for my eyes to adjust. Once they do, they rest on Aaron standing with Angela at his side and then I see a body sitting on the only chair in the room. I know right away it's Julian. I look around till my eyes come to rest on a hole in the door next to Julian and even from this distance, I can see his hand is bleeding. I try to speak but my mouth is too dry and all I want to do is scream at them. Everything hurts and feels so heavy but I manage to lift my arm just enough to bang on the table I'm lying on and a little wince slips through my dry parted lips. Not even a moment later everyone turns to look at me. Aaron and Julian are at my side in the next second.

Aaron puts his hand on my head to rub my hair off my clammy forehead, "How are you feeling?"

Afraid to speak but I try anyway, "Wate-" but the word gets stuck in my mouth as I start to cough.

Next thing I know Angela's there holding my head up and putting a cup to my mouth and helping me drink. She did it so fast and soft that I never even noticed her hand go under my neck and prop me up. When I've had enough water and know I will be ok to talk I look around the room at all the worried faces and despite the pain, I smile trying to reassure them as I say, "I'm just peachy how about all of you?"

Angela smiles back, Julian looks away and Aaron does a halfhearted smile with a sigh.

"I'm fine, just a little sore is all."

"Stop pretending you're only making it worse." I look to see Julian standing by the door, resting against it.

Aaron looks from me to him and back again. "You need to rest."

"Haven't I been sleeping long enough?"

Angela takes my hand then, "You've been asleep for four days but your body still needs more time."

"What! Four days." I almost scream the words out and regret it a moment later as the pain shoots through my body.

Aaron looks at me and closes his eyes, "Your wounds were severe. You were lucky Julian got you here as fast as he did or you never would have had a chance."

Julian laughs from across the room, "Are you kidding me? She wouldn't have to go through any of this if I had been paying closer attention."

I try to sit up and the pain is like fire under my skin and I can't hold back the loud gasp that comes out of my mouth and in a moment everyone is at my side again.

Aaron's eyes almost pop out of his head when he looks at me, "Stop moving, your injuries are still very serious and most of them haven't started to heal yet."

I look at Julian and say, "I'll be damned if I'm going to lay here while he blames himself for it."

Angela and Aaron look at Julian but he won't cut eye contact with me. "So what, I'm just supposed to act like nothing happened and you're fine?"

Julian looks to the ground and I make my face as serious as I can, and I say, "Yes, because this isn't your fault. I walked out, I tried to leave on my own when I knew I wouldn't be able to. I did this, not you, so stop."

"No, I won't stop because it was my responsibility to make sure nothing happened to you and I couldn't even do that." He pauses long enough to lift his hand to gesture at me, "I mean look at you, Amberly." Then he moves his hand behind his head and rustles his hair and I can't help noticing how tragically beautiful he looks as he continues, "That is my fault, mine, not yours."

My voice breaks as I reply, "Please, stop. This wasn't you, there was nothing more you could have done."

When Julian removed his hand from his hair and looks back at me I can see tears forming in his eyes and I feel a pain in my heart as he chokes out, "I can't."

I had forgotten anyone else was in the room with us until Aaron stood in front of me to look at Julian and break our connection, "You will do whatever she wishes. She needs her rest and she is not to be stressed."

Julian looks to the ground and walks away, "If you need anything let me know."

Before I can think of something to say to get him to stay and to make Aaron understand Julian's already out the door and gone from view. His absence is already noticeable to me and I still can't help but question these feelings.

Aaron looks at Angela, "Go make sure he doesn't do anything stupid, please."

With a nod, she walks out of the room after Julian like I wish I could be doing. I should be the one going after him but sadly I'm not in any shape for that. Seconds later I realize now it's only me and Aaron.

"So tell me honestly, how are you feeling?"

I fall back to the bed and close my eyes, "Like bird poop."

I hear Aaron laugh and I can't help but smile. "Bird poop, huh? I'm a little afraid to ask how you know what bird poop feels like."

For the first time, we look at each other and we both start laughing so hard that I have to stop from the pain, and for the first time since Julian told me Aaron was my father, I actually wouldn't mind if it was true.

Chapter 26

J ulian

"She's so stubborn and she drives me crazy." I stop myself short when I see the look on Angela's face, "What?"

She looks away, "Oh, nothing."

I stop dead in my tracks and she follows suit. She turns to look at me and I cross my arms before saying, "What?"

"Who does she remind you of?"

I drop my arms back at my sides, "I don't know."

Angela smiles as she replies, "Don't play dumb." All I can do is smile in reply before she says, "No wonder you have feelings for her, because in a lot of ways she's you but in girl form."

Angela starts to laugh and I don't know if I should be annoyed or laugh with her. I'm happy that Amberly is awake and doing better than she was, but now I have to deal with the very thing I was trying to avoid, my feelings for her.

"I don't know what to do, Angela."

Taken aback she says, "About?"

"About how I feel about her. I know you said we would find a way but honestly, I don't think there is one." I look to my feet before continuing, "And even if there is I don't know if we should try to find it."

"Why not?"

I sigh and move away to look back in the door at Amberly on the bed and her father at her side, "Because I'm not good enough for her."

A little annoyed, Angela says, "Don't do that."

I peel my gaze from the room to look at her and say, "Do what?"

"You're so quick to give up. She makes you happy and that alone is something to fight for."

"It's because she makes me happy and because of my feelings for her, that I want more for her. She deserves better than me."

Annoyed at me she crosses her arms over her chest, "Don't you think that should be her choice?"

"More like it's a choice she shouldn't and won't have to make."

"And how is that fair to anyone?"

I lift my hand to run my fingers through my hair, "Because it would never work out so it would save her the time and the heartache," I lower my hand back to my side before continuing, "We both know how bad I am at the love thing. I would only hurt her and then Aaron would have to kill me so it would be a lose, lose, lose situation for all of us." I look at Angela and smile, trying to make light of the situation, "Her with the broken heart, me with having to try again at something I know there's no point in trying, and also the loss of my life and Aaron would be losing his best pack member." I widen my grin to where I'm showing my teeth in a playful manner but still, Angela doesn't smile.

"You're stupid, you know?"

"Well it's not the first time I've heard it." My smile fades as I say, "But still doesn't make me wrong."

"The best things in life come from the very things we are afraid to take a chance on."

Confused, I stare hard at her, "Meaning?"

Wearing her annoyed face she replies, "Meaning you can sit there and think of reasons to give up, but the bottom line is, you don't know what the outcome would be if you try," she pauses for a moment to take in an annoyed breath and roll her eyes at me, "For all you know it would work out and you could be each other's soul mates and live happily ever after," she throws her hands up in the air so wildly that I take a step back, "But you're a dumb boy and too scared to take the first real chance in your life, so, in the end, you'll be the one losing the most. Not Aaron, and not Amberly, you."

Her words make their way to my ears and I'm frozen. I have no reply. As those words linger in between us, my mind goes a mile a minute thinking. What if she's right? I know Amberly is worth the fight, I just don't think I am. I also don't want her to get hurt and I know how good I am at hurting people. However, Angela's right, it's not just my choice. Without another word, I walk away.

Chapter 27

Aaron

I run right into Angela as I close Amberly's door behind me. My lack of sleep is finally catching up to me. I turn around to face her and smile as I say, "Sorry, I wasn't paying attention."

"You're fine," she replies with a smile of her own, but seconds later it fades. "Are you alright?"

"Honestly, I'm not too sure." The words fall from my lips before I can pull them back. I lift my hand and put it behind my head as I move my hair back and forth. This action used to always calm me but right now it's having no effect.

Angela repeats her question, "What's wrong?"

"It's, Amberly."

Angela's face becomes filled with concern as her gaze moves past me and into the room I left my daughter in. "Is she OK?"

"She's fine." I remove my hand from the back of my head and put it down to my side.

A mask of confusion becomes noticeable on her face, "Then what's wrong?"

"She shouldn't be fine."

Angela's eyes go wide. "What do you mean?"

"She should be dead."

"But she's not. Isn't that a good thing?" The confusion is clear in her eyes.

"Yes, of course, but considering why she is, I don't know."

The skin between her eyebrows crinkles up, "What are you talking about? You're making no sense."

I raise my hand to my face and wipe my eyes feverishly before answering. "What I mean is that the thing around her neck is what healed her, not her wolf blood."

"But either way she's alive so what's the real problem?"

"Something feels wrong about that thing. I remember her mother telling me about it but I didn't think it existed." I reach around to the back of my neck to wipe away at the sweat that's accumulated there, "I need to learn more about it, what if there's a side effect or something bad happens to her because of that thing?" I return my hand to my side, "Magic always comes with a price."

I feel Angela's hand on mine before she says, "And we will but in the meantime your daughter is safe. Concentrate on that."

I shake my head as I turn away and say under my breath, "I wish I could."

"But what could be so dangerous about a necklace?"

I look into her eyes for the first time when I say, "Everything when you know nothing about it. Jocelyn told me about the negative effects of things like that necklace. She told me a story where someone wore a relic their whole life and it protected them from harm and even death. However, she also told me that each time the relic would save that person's life a part of them would fade away and slowly make them crazy or dangerous to others." I look at the door to the room that holds my daughter and I say under my breath, "I don't understand why she would ever give our daughter something like that when she knew herself what it could cost the person."

Angela smiles lightly at me before she replies. "I'm not saying you're wrong but we don't know anything for sure. Maybe she just got lucky and now she's fine."

"I'm telling you Angela, I know her blood, my blood did not heal her."

Angela looks away when she says, "If it was the amulet then what do we do?"

"There's nothing we can do but watch over her and make sure she is completely healed and that it hasn't changed her."

"But how will we know that for sure? She hasn't been here long enough for us to know who she is."

I look at the room that Amberly now lays in and I close my eyes. "The only way to know anything is to talk to the one person who might know more about this."

"And who's that?"

I open my eyes again and look back at Angela as I reply, "Her mother."

Chapter 28

Amberly

It's been one whole week since I woke up after my attack, one whole week since I've seen Julian. Aaron says I'll be fine but that I need rest. The problem is I'm so tired of sitting here and if Julian won't come to see me then I'll just have to go find him.

I feel so dirty in the outfit they changed me into a few days ago. The last one was a little tight so they found me this one. It's a long brown cloth and it's so loose around my shoulders and my hips that when I put my feet on the ground I have to quickly grab the fabric before it slides off my chest. Talk about going from one extreme to the other.

The pain is horrible as I make my way to the door but I fight through it with every step. It's around 6 p.m. and I know this because most of the pack is not in the cave. It's around this time that they leave to go hunting, at the same time every day. The only people I see in the other room are two men I've never met, a woman and Julian. I notice him immediately but I keep my cool. My father told them to make sure I stayed on bed rest so if I went out there it would just cause a scene. So instead I decide to lie back in bed and call out that I'm hungry.

In less than ten seconds one of the male's that I don't know enters my room and bows his head, "How may I serve you, your highness?"

"Well, first you can stop bowing and stop calling me highness." The man stands up straight and I sigh, "Where is Julian?"

The man looks behind him as if in need of assistance, "He is in the other room."

"Well I wish to see him, please."

The man's face turns to one of pain, "I will see if I can do that for you."

I lean back on the bed and fold my arms over my chest and wait.

Ten long minutes later I hear the door open and when I look over I nearly fall off the bed. It's Julian and he looks more beautiful than ever. His chest is showing through the button down shirt he's wearing and the pants are low around his waist and show his navel and hip bones. It's enough to make me fall off the bed but I keep my composure. A second later I feel like I'm hit in the gut hard, as I look at Julian and he bows to me like the other man did, "You called for me your highne-"

I nearly jump off my bed when I scream, "Don't you dare finish that sentence!"

Julian's head flies up, "But that's what you are. You are the daughter of our pack leader and because of that you are to be treated like royalty. That is how a pack works."

"I don't give two flying pigs about the pack rules."

Julian's eyes go wide as I sit up and the blanket falls to my hips. My so-called dress is hanging on my breast by a thread. I look at him as he looks away and I slowly lift the blanket back up, "Please, come here."

He turns to head for the door, "I don't think that's a good idea, someone else can assist you with whatever you may need."

"I asked for you and it's you I want."

Julian stops in his tracks, "Don't say that."

Once my mind registers on what he means I swallow and say with all the confidence I can muster, "But I do want you. You're all I've been able to think about all week. Wondering why you wouldn't come see me and what I could have done wrong but most importantly just thinking about you. You're what I want. "

Before I can form my next words Julian's hand is in my hair and his lips are hot on mine. The passion is more than I can bear so I let out a moan and Julian pulls away, "Did I hurt you?"

I can't help but laugh and as he looks down at me I smile, "No."

"What's so funny?"

"Oh, nothing."

He gets that devilish look on his face that I love so much and says, "OK, fine be that way. If you don't want to tell me I can leave and come back later."

He begins to walk away and I grab him by the back of his shirt, "Don't you dare leave."

I can see all the seriousness and playfulness vanish from his face, "I'm sorry."

Confused, I ask, "Sorry, for what?"

"Many things."

Annoyed and a little curious, I say, "Enlighten me."

"Other than the wolf thing-"

"OK stop right there, that wasn't your fault I'm the one who ran out on my own," I could tell he was about to say something so I put my figure to his lips to silence him, "So there will be no more talk about that. Do you have anything else?"

He shakes his head behind my figure and smiles at me playfully. Once I remove my hand he's serious again, "I shouldn't have kissed you like that."

"And why not?"

"Because you're not mine to be kissing."

In all seriousness now I say, "But what if I want to be?"

When he looks up at me again his eyes are sparkling and I can see the happiness lingering in them, wanting to come out but unsure. "Don't play with me, please."

"I'm not."

He leans back and away from me, "So what are you saying?"

"I thought it was obvious, at least I thought you were smart enough to figure it out." I smile.

He lifts his hand to my face and I close my eyes to his touch. "So if I was to touch you like this?"

I open my eyes to meet his again and I test out my theory about being about to hear each other in human form when I say, *I would beg for you not to stop.*

His eyes go wide but that's not how I know for sure that he's heard me. His lips are forceful on mine again and his other hand is tight on my back pressing me against him. Within moments my thoughts aren't my own. I can hear him as he can hear me calling out to him.

I hear him think, *You're so beautiful,* and moments later, *You don't know how hard it has been for me to stay away from you.*

And I reply, *then don't.*

He lays me back down on the bed while never-ending our kiss. Within moments he is on top of me and our kissing intensifies. His tongue encircles mine as it sends chills through my body, as his hands, hard against my hip, send chills down my spine. Wanting him to touch me and never stop I lift my hands to go around him and pull him closer to me. I feel his body get hard and I let go of him. Moments later he lifts his head away from me.

I sit up, "Are you OK? What's wrong?"

"Give me a second."

I lift my hand to his cheek and turn his face to meet my eyes and I see his are closed, "Open your eyes."

"Give me a minute."

"Please, open them."

Reluctantly he opens his eyes and I muffle a gasp. The whole outside of his eyes are now black, the inside is a light blue, and they are glowing, "Are you ok? What's wrong with your eyes?"

Hesitantly, he says, pulling away, "It's a long story."

I can feel how much he needs to be away from me right now, while I want him as close as possible. He sits next to me dropping his face in his hands as I lay my hand on his back. I can tell something is bothering him but I don't know what, "I'm listening."

He lets out a sigh before he starts, "My father told me a story a very long time ago about a legend. I didn't think it was at all true till now."

I sit there patiently waiting for him to continue and just when I think he won't, "He said when people of our kind get together a shift can happen." He pauses to look in my direction before he continues, "He told me it hadn't happened for hundreds of years, but you'll know when your eyes start to change and you would feel it happening."

"Did it hurt?"

He shakes his head, "No."

"So this is something that's happened before? Has it happened to you before now? I mean when you've been with someone before?"

He turns to look at me and I know he's making his facial expression as serious as possible so I know he's not lying when he says, "No, it's never happened, not before this, not before you."

"What does that mean?"

He looks away from me again and I can see in his eyes that he's debating whether or not to tell me everything, "He told me that this only happens with our kind when we find the person we are meant to be with for the rest of our lives."

I continue to look at him waiting to hear the rest. I know if I interrupt him I'll never get the whole story.

Still looking away from me he continues, "He said something about it meaning you and the other person are foreordained. I don't know what that means exactly, but all I do know is he told me it hadn't happened in a very long time and I don't know if this is what is going on but it feels like it." He turns to look at me and all the happiness I saw before is gone from his eyes, "I need to do right by you and this isn't right."

"What are you talking about?"

He looks from me to the bed we are sitting on, "This. This isn't right. And now everyone will know."

"It doesn't matter what they know."

"Yes, it does." He turns away from me before continuing, "Your father will not be happy."

I almost yell, but I calm myself before I speak, "I don't care what my father thinks," I put my hands on his cheeks to make him look at me, "I've never felt this way about anyone before. I want to be with you." Logan creeps into my head but only for a moment.

He removes my hands from his face and looks away, "Not like this."

"We didn't do anything wrong. We didn't have sex. We care for each other; I don't see how that can be wrong?"

He slides himself off the bed, still not looking my way, "It's not wrong. It's how I feel about you. It could never be wrong."

"Then what is?"

I hear him release a sigh, "I'm not right for you."

In a second I'm off the bed and standing before him, "Don't you ever think that."

"But I'm not. Your father and everyone in the pack know it."

I shake my head profusely, "I don't care what they think-"

"You need to because without their approval we can't be together. I shouldn't even be in here right now." He turns to walk away and I grab him by the arm.

"Don't go."

He turns back to face me, "You don't understand. Because you are his daughter you need to be mated to the right wolf and to them, I'm not the right one."

He can see the disgust on my face I'm sure because his lips curl into a smile.

Without thinking I stand on my tiptoes and I throw my arms around his neck and begin to kiss him. At first he doesn't kiss back whether because of the surprise or something else I'm not sure, but then I feel his arms go tight around me as he kisses me back.

In moments my back is against the wall and his hands are on my hips. After some time he pulls away again and rests his forehead against mine. We are both panting hard.

"We need to stop doing that," he says between pants.

"Why? Don't you want to kiss me?"

"Of course I do. Every minute of every day I would."

"Then why do we need to stop? I felt it when you kissed me. I know you feel like I do."

His hand is on my cheek so fast I don't have time to think, "I feel more for you than you could ever know. You have awakened something in me. I don't know how to explain it but this isn't me. I'm not this kind of person normally. But you, you make me want to be better. In every sense of the word, you've saved me. But kissing you is wrong and it's only getting harder to not kiss you the longer we are together."

"Then why stop?"

I pull him down to me again and this time he doesn't resist at all but instead slides his tongue through my lips as he grabs me by the butt and lifts me around his waist. For a moment we sit there against the wall making out and then he carries me back to the bed and lays me down. After a few minutes he ends our kiss and he is panting again. I can't help but smile at him.

He looks down at me as he smiles back, "I have to go now. Before I can't make myself leave."

"And what would be so wrong with that?"

My facial expression makes him smile, "You seduce me, my lady and I like it. But I must leave before I do something we will regret later."

I wrinkle up my nose, "My lady?"

He bends down to kiss me on the forehead, "Yup. Sleep well."

Both a little disappointed and tired I lay down as I watched him leave the room. In minutes I'm falling asleep with a smile on my face.

Chapter 29

A mberly

"Amberly!"

The sound of my name rings through my head. Not wanting to wake up I grab the pillow from under my head and throw it over my face as I sigh. Thoughts of last night make me smile, hoping it wasn't just a dream. But the smile doesn't last long.

"Amberly!"

This time the voice is louder and closer. I shoot upright out of bed when I realize I recognize the voice. I throw the pillow off of me as I look around. Aaron and Angela are lying on cots across the room from me. I wonder how they are still asleep as the yelling continues from outside the cave.

I grab a handful of the blanket and yank it off me as I jump out of the bed and as I land on my feet I notice all the pain I've been feeling from the attack is gone. I look down and see that most of the cuts and bruises have faded away as well.

"Amberly, where are you?"

Logan's voice rings through the cave and I see Aaron starting to stir in the cot across from me and know I need to move fast. I grab my coat and shoes from in front of the door and make my way outside.

I spot Troy and Logan about fifty feet from the cave opening as I make my way down the stony path to meet them, trying to duck the best I can so they don't see me coming. I don't know why really but I feel like they shouldn't know about the cave or the pack, at least not yet.

Only a few feet from them, they have their backs to me, I take this chance to take them by surprise, "Hey, there you guys."

Logan turns around so fast that it almost gives me whiplash. I open my mouth to say something else but before I get the chance he's closed the distance between us and has his arms tightly around me. I smile as I hug him back.

"Where have you been? No, scratch that, why the hell did you leave the village?" I can hear the annoyance in his voice, so I don't need to see the look on his face to know he isn't happy with me.

Moments later he ends our embrace and steps back, "Well?"

Before I can think of a reply Troy opens his mouth, "Easy, she's crazy and has a death wish that's why?"

"Still mad about me whipping your ass I see. How's it feel when you get beat by a girl? I wonder how you'll ever live that down." I say with a smile on my face.

I look back at Logan and see his face change as his eyes look me up and down and he moves his hand to cup my chin and then turns my face to the side.

"What happened to you?"

I grab his hand. "I'm fine, it's nothing, just took a hard fall."

He looks at me unsure and sighs. "OK. We need to get going."

My smile fades and I don't know what to say.

"What's wrong?" Logan says as he puts his hand on my arm.

I look up at him and force a smile, "Nothing. How's my mom?"

"Oh, she's great. Not worried at all." Troy says with a smile. I look away from him.

Logan's face is a mask. I don't know what he's thinking but before I can ask I'm in his arms again. "God, I missed you."

I smile and embrace him once more while resting my cheek on his shoulder, "I missed you too."

He pulls back to where our faces are only two inches apart. I see him look at my lips in question like he's confused about something. He begins to lean in and I freeze. Before Julian, I would never have hesitated in kissing Logan but now I'm not so sure. It's like a part of me wants Logan and another part wants Julian and suddenly I'm angry. I feel his lips brushing mine but before they make complete contact Troy yells, "OK, come on now. We've been away from home long enough and we have a long walk back so we should probably be on our way. You guys can talk on the way."

Normally this would piss me off and I would say something snotty to him but right now I'm thankful for his annoying interruption. I pull away a little further and smile at Logan. His face is one of need and I feel like I just stomped on that. Trying to hide it he smiles at me not knowing it's too late. He looks down at my hand questioningly. I know what he's asking so I take his hand in mine and pull him along after Troy on the road home.

And I get the feeling we aren't alone.

Chapter 30

Julian

As I watch them in the distance something tightens in my stomach.

The way he holds her.

I hear myself growling under my breath and realize my lips are pulled back in a snarl and I have to correct myself. Seeing her with him awakens something dark within me. A part of me that has disappeared since she has come to the cave but now watching her embrace him like a long lost lover makes me that person once again.

It takes everything in me not to jump off the top of the cave to the ground below and rip his heart out just for touching her.

And then it gets worse.

I can see the look in his eyes even from this distance and I catch myself growling once more except this time I don't stop.

I can't stop.

As he leans in she doesn't move and I begin to ask myself why?

Does she love him? Does she want him? Or is it just confusion?

She has awakened something in me that I've never felt before. It's more than a need for her, it's almost like she's been with me all my life and I'm not only now meeting her. It feels like she's always been mine even when she wasn't and now seeing this just makes me want to fight more for what I can feel deep down is what I was always meant to have.

Her.

I see their lips brush slightly before they are pulled apart and I'm livid.

The hatred for this man I've never met is so great and I can't control it. I look down to see my hands are shaking and my nails have grown out to claws.

I look once more in their direction and smile.

Chapter 31

Amberly

"So how's my mom really?"

Troy smiles at me before answering my question. "She's great. The fact that her only daughter ran off by herself into the forest didn't faze her at all."

"You're a dick you know that?"

"Yea, but that's what you love about me," Troy says as he closes his eyes and makes kissy lips in my direction.

I turn in Logan's direction, completely annoyed.

"Why did you leave on your own?" Logan says without looking in my direction.

"I wanted to get out for a while."

"But by yourself after what happened with the wolves? That's not like you."

"I had to figure something out."

Logan stops and turns on me. "Like what? What was so important that you couldn't wait for me to go with you? Or ask me to at least."

I turn away before answering. "You don't understand."

"Damn right I don't so why don't you explain it to me."

"Why don't we continue this when we get home? We aren't that far." Troy smiles and continues, "Because I for one don't want another encounter with wolves right now. Plus, you guys have been talking, or maybe I should say arguing, for the last few days I think you guys could use a brake."

It's hard to believe how short the walk home was since it felt like Julian ran forever when he brought me to the cave. I mean it was a few days walk but with how fast he ran I really thought it would have been a longer journey. Maybe he ran in circles or something to throw me off, to make sure I didn't know how to get home or how to return once I did. Well, now I know the way.

Logan looks away from me. "You're right, let's keep walking."

* * *

Julian

I enter the cave to see Aaron and Angela sitting up in their cots talking in hushed tones. The anger still lingers in my body as I approach them. I try not to let them see it as they both look up at me and smile.

"Good morning, Julian. You're up early, it's not even sunrise." Angela says.

Aaron's smile fades after looking at me for a moment then he stands. "What is it?"

"Amberly she's gone."

Angela stands and grabs Aaron by the wrist while still looking at me. "What do you mean gone? Where did she go?"

"Her humans came to collect her."

Aaron's eyes go wide. "Did they enter the cave?"

"No, she must have heard them outside and got up and went to meet them. When I found her she was outside the cave entrance with them."

"So she left to protect the identity of the cave and the sleeping wolves inside?" Aaron says looking relieved.

"I don't think that's why she went with them."

Angela turns her gaze away from Aaron to look at me. "Then why?"

"I think she is in love with one of the humans. I could overhear their conversation and they talked to one another like lovers that have been separated for too long."

Angela's face drops even more. I wonder then if it's because of the conversation she and I had about my feelings for Amberly or if it's for some other reason. Maybe because Aaron's only child, only heir, could be in love with someone not of our kind.

Aaron pulls his arm out of Angela's hold and with it our attention. "She will come back. She was protecting the cave and the pack, I'm sure of it." Then he turns and walks away. Angela follows but not before looking in my direction one more time.

Chapter 32

Amberly

My feet are planted in the dirt and don't want to move. My body refuses to take another step and honestly I'm glad. Knowing I'm moments away from having my mom standing in front of me makes my body stiffen.

What will I say to her?

All this time she believed my father was dead. Or did she? What if she knew he was alive all this time and just didn't want me to know about him or what I am? How can I face her when I don't know if I want her answers? How am I supposed to be the one to tell her that all these years she was wrong and my father is alive?

"Amberly!"

I look up to see my mother running towards me. I don't know what to do as my body continues to stand in the same spot, frozen. I can tell by the way she looks that she hasn't been doing much in my absence. Her dark hair is flying all over the place and looks like it hasn't been brushed since I left. Her dark grey pants and shirt have stains all over the front and it makes me shutter at the thought of her wearing things like this in my absence. And if she's wearing that now then god only knows what she was wearing all the other days while I was gone.

Don't get me wrong I don't dress my mother but sometimes she wants to wear certain things that I don't agree with and I will always talk her out of wearing them. However, with me not being here I don't know how much damage she's done.

In the next moment, I'm in her arms and she's squeezing me tight.

"Thank God you're OK. I was so worried."

"Were you?"

She pulls away to look into my eyes. "How could you even ask that? Of course, I was worried."

"Like you were about dad?"

Her smile is torn off her face as she looks away. "What does this have to do with your father?"

"Everything."

I can see her roll her eyes at me before she turns her head away and says, "Enlighten me, please. Because you've been gone a long time and I don't know where you went or why."

"I went to get answers to all the questions I had. After you refused to give them to me."

"What answers?"

"Who I am for starters."

My mother's face is taken over by a look of hurt when she replies, "You're, Amberly Grayson and my daughter."

"That's not what I mean and you know it. You've known it all along and said nothing."

She turns her back to me and continues. "You don't know what you are talking about. Let's go inside now."

"See this is what I'm talking about. This is why I left to find answers because this is always your answer. Nothing." I say as I cross my arms over my chest and let out an annoyed sigh.

"I don't want to talk about this, not right now. We will continue this conversation later. What's more important is you're alright but there will be consequences for you leaving like you did."

"You never want to talk about anything when I want to, it's always when you want to."

She looks to the ground and closes her eyes. "That's because I'm the parent and you're the child."

"I'm guessing you haven't looked at me recently because I'm not a child anymore and what does being a parent have to do with me getting the answers I deserve?"

My mother lifts her head once more to look me in the eyes and I can feel the coldness in them. "You're not a child? Then stop acting like one. The way you talk and the way you just took off without a word. That's what a child would do and that's what you did so what does that make you?"

I shake my head furiously before answering her. "It doesn't make me a child, it makes me someone who wants answers and will do anything to get them. Including pissing you off, that's just a bonus."

Her eyes go wide at my response. "Who are you? I know we have always had our problems and we aren't as close as I would like but this isn't like you."

"Maybe I'm tired of all the lies Mom. Ever think about that? And you still haven't answered my question like normal."

Now it's her turn to shake her head from side to side as her free hair bobs up and down on her shoulders. "Answer to what question?"

I let out a repressed sigh while trying not to show my annoyance. "The one where you being the parent has nothing to do with me getting the truth."

"It doesn't really but...I guess ask. What is it you want to know? Although for the record I would much rather do this inside."

Not caring where she wants to talk, I plant my feet in the dirt and don't plan on moving an inch when I ask. "Who was my father?"

"I told you more times than I can count that he was the best man I've ever known."

"That's not what I'm asking."

"Ok, then be more clear with your question because honestly I don't get what you're asking me."

I press my lips together and out trying to stop myself from screaming at her. I count to ten before I say another word. "I'm asking you who he was...what he was."

I can see her eyes trying to hide what she knows and it infuriates me. "I don't know what you mean."

"Ok. Fine, I know he wasn't from our village so where did you meet him?"

Her eyes get so wide that her eyebrows become part of her hairline. "How do you know that?"

"Don't worry about it, just answer the question, please."

"Your father and I met in the woods. He was from another village."

"Ok, and what was that village?"

I can see her eyes begin to shut down and I know she's about to close herself off again, with all the secrets I already know the answers to, locked inside. "We should go inside now and maybe get you something to eat and then we can continue this conversation."

"Well, there's another lie," I say almost under my breath so I'm a little surprised when she hears me.

"Just come inside and we will continue this later."

As she walks back towards our home I don't move. I close my eyes and say, "No, we won't because I won't be here."

She turns back around to look at me with anger plastered all over her face as it turns a dark shade of scarlet. "Excuse me?"

"You heard me. I'm leaving."

She crosses her arms over her chest to mimic my annoyance. Now I see where I get it from and all it's doing is making me madder than I already am.

"And where do you plan to go?"

"To my dad."

I can see her eyes fill with tears as she turns away from me again. "Your father is dead and I don't want to talk about this anymore."

She starts to walk back into our home but my words stop her. "No, he's not."

Chapter 33

Amberly

"It's not possible. He died before you were born."

My mother continued to say the same thing over and over as she paced back and forth.

"Mom, is there a chance that you were wrong?"

"No...No, I know what I saw."

"And what is that?"

I can see the lines on her face deepen as she tries to recall the memory from so many years ago. "Your father was lying on the ground covered in blood. He wasn't moving."

"But are you sure that he was dead?"

She turns to look at me with a river running down her face. "I felt it. My heart broke as I looked at his unmoving body broken on the ground. I knew he was gone."

"But did you check?"

I could see the water starting to form in the corner of her eyes and I feel horrible for making her relive the memory but it's the only way. The only way she would believe what I was about to tell her. "I…I couldn't."

"Why?"

"I…You said he's not dead, what does that mean?"

I close my eyes before I can answer her. "I met him when I was in the woods."

"But how do you know it was him for sure?"

I tuck my hands in my pants pockets and say, "Because he has the same name and he looked the way you told me he did, and when I said who I was and who my mother was the rest of the pack reacted to it but let's just say his reaction was the easiest to notice."

Her eyes come to focus back on me once mine open. "How do you know about the pack?"

"I was there with him, remember?"

"What I mean is how did you come across him, your father? It's not like he's close."

"I met someone in the woods when me and Troy and Logan went out."

She turns her eyes to the door as she starts to think, hard. "But how the only person, I mean thing, you saw was the wolf…at least that's what the boys said."

"And they didn't lie, that's all I did see."

"Then how?" The realization is so alive in her eyes, "You know what you are then?"

"I know I have shapeshifter blood in me if that's what you mean? I kind of knew something was off when I could hear the wolf talking in my head and Logan couldn't."

"I…where is he?"

"The wolf?" I say, confused.

"No, your father."

Knowing I won't get any more answers from her I decide to answer her question. "He's in the woods, with the other wolves."

Her face doesn't show any surprise and that's when I know for sure.

"You always knew what he was didn't you?"

She looks up at me with tear-filled eyes. "Yes."

"And you never thought to tell me?"

"I was going to when you were older."

"Bullshit."

Her eyes go wide with surprise, "Watch your mouth."

I throw my hands into the air as I spin away from her. "Why should I? I don't owe you anything. You lied to me about everything for my whole life. You lied to me about who I really am."

"I was trying to protect you."

"From what?'

She stands as she replies. "Everything."

"Hey, how is everything?" I hear Logan's voice come from the threshold of the hut.

I lift my hand to wipe away the tears that had escaped my eyes moments before, "We're good but I'm leaving."

I don't have to look at him to know he has a look of confusion plastered on his face. "What do you mean you're leaving?"

"I'm going back." I say as I turn around to face him.

"To the woods?"

"Yes, I know it sounds crazy but once you know everything it will make sense."

I turn away from Logan and my mom and walk into my room and grab some clothes and other things I will need and throw them in a bag as they watch me.

I grab my brush and Logan grabs my wrist and whispers, "What's going on, Amberly?"

"I can't explain it right now."

"Well, you aren't going anywhere till you do."

I throw my brush in the bag and look into his eyes and know he's serious. I let out a long breath in anticipation of what I'm about to tell him. "My father…he's alive."

Logan's jaw drops open as he turns to look at my mom and then back to me. "Are you sure?"

"I've met him."

Chapter 34

Amberly

It's amazing how quickly everything changed after that. All Logan could do was stare at me, unsure of what to say next, my mother wouldn't stop yelling at me, and then as Logan decided to leave the hut, trying to give me and my mother time to talk things over, he runs into Troy and of course, he had to know what was going on. After talking with everyone my mother, Logan, and Troy all packed a bag of their own and said they would go with me. However, they all refused to leave until the next morning.

My heart races as I lay in my bed looking at the ceiling thinking of my father, Julian and Angela. It's crazy how easy it is to miss someone that you barely know and I'd be lying if I said it didn't scare me a little that I'm already calling Aaron my dad, especially since I barely know anything about him and vice versa. As I lie awake in my white spaghetti strap tank top and my thin white shorts I become very aware of Logan lying in my bed next to me and I think about how he doesn't know about Julian and Julian doesn't know about him.

I let out a repressed sigh as I leaned my head back against the cold wall and close my eyes hoping for sleep. It's seconds before I'm caught off guard once more and my heart skips a beat as Logan's arm is thrown over my torso. I look over to see him sound asleep with a smile on his face.

I don't understand how it can feel so right here with him and so right with Julian in the cave. The difference with Julian is the future is unknown but the feelings are overwhelming. Whereas with Logan it's so easy to love him. I grew up with him and we know each other like the backs of our hands whereas I don't know much about Julian. It is like I'm being split in two. One part wants to be with Julian and the wolves and the other wants to be here with Logan.

As I lay here looking at him I miss the feeling of normal and I know nothing will ever be the same or normal again and suddenly it feels like something is missing. Logan begins to snuggle in close as the front of his face comes to rest on my rib and his nose pokes me in the side. His arm travels to my belly button as he grabs a fistful of my tank top. I used to be embarrassed when any of my skin would show but now lying here with him and his hand knotted up in my shirt it doesn't bother me at all. I can't help but smile at how innocent he looks while he is asleep. His eyes open slowly and he looks like he's a little unsure of where he is at first but then his eyes make contact with mine as I smile at him. He starts to smile back but then his eyes catch his hand knotted up in my tank top as it starts to show a little too much skin. His cheeks start to blush as he looks away from me and retracts his hand and arm from my body. And suddenly I'm cold.

I start to pull my shirt back down and Logan's eyes catch the last bit of flesh showing before it's covered again. He looks away before saying a word. "I'm sorry, did I wake you?"

I smile down at him. "No, I've been up."

"You should get some sleep."

I look up at the ceiling as I lean my head back against the wall. "I know I've been trying, really I have."

He leans up to lay his head on his hand as his elbow makes a dent in the bed. "What's wrong?"

"Nothing."

"Amberly, you forget I know you." He smiles before he continues, "I know you're thinking about something. What is it?"

I turn my head sideways to look at him. "Seeing my dad again, my mom and dad seeing each other for the first time in years. It's weird and crazy but in a good way. I'm wondering what will happen from here."

"What do you mean?"

I look at the ceiling once more. "Like will we all come to live here or will my mom and I move there with him?"

"Where does he live?"

I pause unsure if I should tell him everything.

"Amberly?"

"I need to tell you something but I need you to promise you won't think I'm crazy or look at me any differently."

He straightens up and knocks the pillow off the bed as he does so. "I promise."

I pull my attention away from the ceiling as I straighten my body in the bed to look at him better. "My dad, well he's kind of a shapeshifter."

"What do you mean?"

"You know how we can move things with our minds and control certain elements and stuff?"

He nods his head and I continue. "Well, he can change his form. He can turn into a wolf."

He sits up completely in the bed now. "So does that mean...you're part wolf?"

It takes me a minute to answer as my eyes wander over his chest as moisture starts to build in between his pecs. Thankfully I removed my eyes from the area before he noticed I was even looking. "Yes, that's why the wolves acted weird when we were in the woods. The one wolf he...he was talking to me."

"What?"

He's quiet for a moment and when I realize that's all he's going to say I decide to end the silence. "The 'what' was to which part," I say with a smile.

"Oh, ya sorry...All of it really but I mean why didn't you tell me about the wolf thing before?"

"I'm sorry. To be honest I was a little afraid of what you would think of me when I told you. I mean sometimes I think I've gone a little nuts myself so I couldn't really blame you if you thought the same."

Logan places his hand on top of my right one and his smile disappears as he becomes all serious. "I could never think you were crazy."

Looking into his eyes makes me realize without a doubt how lucky I have been and how lucky I am that we will always be friends.

Logan releases my hand and smiles. "So this talking to the wolf thing?"

"It's hard to explain. I was able to hear him in my head. He told me I had wolf blood in me and that's why I left. I needed answers that I knew I couldn't get here."

"And that's when you met your dad?"

"Yes."

Logan moves closer to me on the bed, close enough to make the hair on my arms stand up from the warmth of his body next to my cold one. "How are you feeling about all of this?"

I look away as I lean back on the bed and pull the covers up to my chin. "It feels good. I mean it's still confusing and there's still a lot I don't know. But a few weeks ago I didn't have a father and I felt like there was something I didn't know about myself and now...now I have a father and I know what I didn't know before."

"Does any of it scare you?"

I pause for a moment to really think about his question and about my answer, "Yes. Everything does. There is still so much I don't know and so much I need to learn about the wolf or shapeshifter part of myself."

"Have you shifted at all yet?"

My eyes go wide as I shake my head to the side to give my answer.

"I'm sorry. Maybe I shouldn't have asked."

"No, it's just that...I don't know anything about that part of me yet...It scares me that I don't know when or how it will happen. All I know about the shapeshifters is that they can turn into wolves. But when it comes to how or when or if it will hurt..." Logan moves closer to me and puts his arm around my shoulders and pulls me in close. "That I know nothing about," I say into his bare chest.

"I'm sorry. I wish I had known and been there for you more. I promise to be here now and to help you find the answers. There will be nothing you don't know when we are done."

I pull away from him to see a smile on his face and I know he's serious about helping me and I've never felt luckier to have him as my friend.

Logan turns to lean off the bed to retrieve his shirt. The bottom half of his body is still on the bed with me and the other is leaning on the floor. "Sorry, I just figured I should put it on."

"If you're hot you don't have to."

"You sure?"

I smile before answering. "Yes, I'm not a little girl and you're not making me uncomfortable or anything."

"OK, then." He says as he tries to push himself back up on the bed and that's when I see it. I almost forgot. The birthmark is staring me right in the face. His is on his back just above his pants line. It's the same color pink and same raven shape as mine, Troy's, and now Angela's. I used to think it was weird that Troy, Logan and I all had the same birthmark even if they were all in different places with little differences, it was still a little creepy.

"Logan?"

He turns his body to face me once he is safely back on the bed. "Yea?"

"Did you ever find it weird that you, me and Troy all have the same birthmark?"

The corner of his mouth creeps up to meet his eye. "Not really. I kind of took it as a sign that we were all meant to be friends."

"Well, what if I tell you one of the wolves in my father's pack has the same one?"

Chapter 35

Amberly

We are only a few miles from the cave and I can feel my stomach growing tight with anticipation. Since I left I've been waiting to see Julian and my father again, like I left a part of me behind.

Julian. I didn't tell Logan about him and I never told Julian about Logan either. *What a pickle I've gotten myself into this time.* Then to make matters worse there is the way I feel about them both, *man how confusing these feelings are,* and then there is the whole birthmark thing. Logan and I didn't talk much about it. He just kept asking if I was sure I saw what I thought I saw and when I said yes he just said it was a coincidence. The funny thing is I don't believe in those. I know something deeper going on because there is no way a handful of people would have the same birthmark let alone from two different villages. I can feel this need or urge to figure out what these marks can mean. It feels like if I can find out the truth behind them things might finally start to fall into place in my life, and yes I know how weird that sounds.

I look up and see the entrance to the cave. I hadn't realized we walked this far already. I feel my feet plant themselves in the hard dirt under them as I come to a stop and Logan walks into the back of me.

"You ok?"

I turn around and as his eyes meet mine I answer, "Honestly, I don't know."

Logan lifts his hand to lay it on the upper part of my arm. "It'll be fine."

I turn away from him and look to the ground. "I'm not worried about me. I've already been with him for a few weeks but my mom…they haven't seen each other in eighteen years. What if it doesn't go well?" I pause, unsure if I want to continue, "Or worse what if it goes too well?"

Logan's face turns to one of bewilderment. "What do you mean? Wouldn't that be a good thing? Don't you want it to go well?"

"Not if it takes me away from the only home I've known my whole life and away from you."

Logan smiles and moves his hand to cup my cheek. I close my eyes at his touch and lean into it, so familiar.

"There you are."

Oh no.

I turn around to see Julian standing at the cave entrance with his arms crossed over his chest and a pissed-off look in his eyes. Logan looks from me to Julian and back again while my eyes and Julian's never leave each other.

"Who is that?" Logan asks.

I sigh then answer, "That's Julian."

"Who?"

Julian turns his gaze to Logan, "Oh, so I see she didn't tell you about me."

Logan looks at me with a questioning look and as I look at him Julian descends the rock wall. Before I get the chance to say anything Julian steps in front of me to face Logan.

"So who might you be, mate?"

Logan's eyebrows raise and I have to stop a smile as they nearly meet his hairline. "My name isn't 'mate' I can tell you that much."

I didn't think Julian could look angrier than he already was but I was wrong. I look down to see both of their hands turn into fists at their sides.

"So who do we have here?" Troy says as he pulls Logan back just enough to stand in front of him and face Julian head-on. But Julian's eyes never leave Logan.

"Um, hello. I'm talking to you." Troy says as he pokes Julian in the chest.

I wish he hadn't done that.

Julian lifts his hand to swat away Troy's from his chest, almost like he's a pesky gnat in his way. As Julian's hand smacks Troy's everything goes quiet and Troy looks ready to fight.

Julian removes his eyes from Logan to rest on his new annoyance. "I wouldn't touch me if I were you."

"I didn't ask for your opinion now did I?"

"If you wouldn't mind I would like to talk to Amberly." Julian turns his back to Troy and Logan and grabs me by the wrist.

"Like hell," Logan says before he pushes Julian off me.

Julian turns fast on Logan. "I know I told your friend not to touch me but maybe you didn't get the message."

"I got it loud and clear."

"Then why would you do something so stupid," Julian says with a devilish grin plastered on his face.

Logan never moves his gaze from Julian as he lifts his arm and points in my direction. "You will not touch her like that again."

"I'll touch her however I like whenever I like...mate."

They both look so pissed that I swear I can see little balloons of steam hanging above their heads. Everyone told me about Julian and his temper and past, even he did but I never saw it so I never believed it and as for Logan I've never seen him get mad before and definitely not like this.

"Amberly, let's go," Logan says without looking at me.

"She isn't going anywhere until I talk to her."

Logan reaches out his hand to me and I'm stuck. I don't know what to do. Should I go talk to Julian or go with Logan?

Before I have the chance to decide Julian swats Logan's hand away and moves past him to reach me and then puts his hand behind my back and pushes me forward.

"I said don't touch her," Logan screams and when I turn around I see him charging towards us.

Julian nudges me to the side just in time to take the hit from Logan to the gut. Logan wraps himself around Julian's midsection and pushes back. Julian just lifts his hands up over his head and looks at me and smiles.

"Guys stop it," I scream at them but it doesn't help as they start swinging at each other and then Julian takes Logan to the ground as he charges him and grabs him around the waist.

"Troy, stop them." I look over at Troy with his hands crossed over his chest looking at them.

"Why? It's so much fun watching...plus Logan just got on top."

I turn around to see Troy is right, Logan is now on top of Julian and he's about to punch him in the face again.

I run over to them and grab at Logan's shirt but it's no use. "You guys please stop."

I've lost count of how many punches each had connected with the other's face but looking at them I know Logan got the brunt of it. He has a dark red patch forming on his jaw and just under his hairline as well as a bloody lip. I watch the blood begin to trickle down his chin and I have to look away. Julian however has a little blood running from his nose and that's all. I feel a tug at my heart as I watch them continue to fight and know I have no way to stop them. Or do I ? I remember some of the things Logan was teaching me a few weeks back. I close my eyes and take in a slow deep breath and when I hear my heart slow I open them again and turn my attention to the boys as

I focus on pulling them away from each other with my mind. I can feel it start to work but then someone's hands move me to the side. For a moment I think maybe it's my mom but when I turn around I can see my mom and our two bodyguards still ten feet away from me so I look up and there I find my father. He lightly pushes me back away from the boys. I move to the side as he snatches Logan off Julian and Julian stands up as he whips the blood from his nose with the back of his sleeve with a smile still on his face.

Aaron looks from Julian to Logan with confusion. "Now what was that all about?"

Julian looks away from everyone and out at the forest. "Nothing. Don't worry about it."

"Don't worry about it. You just started a fight in front of the..." Aaron stops short as he looks past us. I turn around to see what made him stop cold. It was my mom, his eyes had finally come to rest on her.

They both stand there and look at each other for what feels like forever. Looking at them it's almost like they can't see anything else but each other at this moment. A moment they thought would never come again. Aaron drops the boys and starts to close the distance between them, slowly at first and then he quickens the pace. I can feel a smile spreading across my face as I turn away.

Chapter 36

Aaron

It feels almost like waking up from a dream. As my eyes come to rest on her I can feel my heart skip a beat but it's more like it's finally starting up again. Almost like it stopped for these last eighteen years and now it's alive again, I'm alive. I can't stop my feet from moving towards her or my arms from rising to cup her face in my hands as tears run down her cheeks. I brush them away silently with my thumbs. I'm unsure what to say to her or if there are even any words that could describe this moment and how it feels to have her in my arms again. So I do the only other thing I can. I pull her hard and fast into me and kiss her.

Not kissing her for years was the hardest thing and now it's like everything is falling back into place and it's all lining up where it was always meant to. I'm a firm believer that everything happens for a reason and up to this point no matter how hard I tried I couldn't justify the loss I endured eighteen years ago. But now, I can say it was all worth it because it brought me here, brought us here.

I feel her body go from tense to limp as my lips touch hers. I remember the feeling of her like it was yesterday and I remember so many other things about her and so I know this is a good sign. I move my arms around her body to pull her closer to me as her hands move around my neck and into my hair.

She pulls back for a second but only to catch her breath and then she's pulling me to her once more but this time it's for a more forceful kiss. One that's so full of all the years we have been separated, of all the passion and long nights without each other. This time I have to pull away and cup her face in my hands to keep her at bay so I can breathe.

I smile and a laugh escapes my open lips as she smiles back at me. She takes my hand in hers and nothing else matters to me as we walk off to the cave entrance together. I know I should be dealing with the boys and saying hello to my daughter and getting everyone settled in, introduced and fed but I just can't take my eyes off the woman I love. The woman I haven't seen in so many years, the woman I thought was dead and lost to me forever and the mother of my child.

* * *

Amberly

I turn away from my parents as they make their way into the cave together. I find my eyes resting on the three boys who continue to glare at each other. I look to the ground as I let out a sigh and shake my head from side to side.

What am I going to do with them?

Julian looks over at me and that's when I remember he can hear anything I say when he concentrates on it and for once I wish I knew how to do it. He turns away and stalks off into the cave after my mom and dad. I'm still looking after him when Logan comes to stand in front of me blocking my view.

"We need to talk."

I look at the ground again and let out another long breath. "I know."

We stand there for a while, neither of us breaking the silence.

"I kind of meant now." I look up to see Logan wearing his serious face and I know it's time I told him everything.

"Fine. You remember the wolf in the woods?"

"The one that you said told you about you being part wolf?"

"Yes." I can't help but pause because I don't know what to say next but I can see Logan is trying to wait patiently for me to continue as he lifts his hand to his face and wipes at his tired-looking eyes.

I close my eyes as I say, "Well, that was him."

Logan's eyes get a little wider as he looks at me and I notice Troy looking off in the direction that Julian disappeared in. Logan is the first one to break the silence, "So he was the wolf that you left with?"

"Yes."

Confusion is still plain on Logan's face as he chooses his next words, "OK. But that still doesn't explain why he was grabbing at you or why he acted that way towards me."

"That's a longer story."

"OK, well I would like to hear it. I'm trying to understand what happened while you were gone all that time. Why didn't you tell me about him and what did I just walk into?"

"It's complicated."

Troy speaks up for the first time then and I couldn't be happier for the distraction. "Wow, man. You just took on a wolf. Hope he doesn't come back and bite you." He pauses to look at me as his face changes from one of enjoyment to one of concern. "If he bites us we won't change into a wolf too will we?"

Or not. "I honestly don't know. Like I told Logan last night, I haven't had much time to learn anything."

"Oh, man we're in deep shit. You just pissed off a werewolf man."

Logan looks over at Troy before he replies. "Not without some help from you, man."

I look back and forth between them when I say, "He's not a werewolf, he's a shapeshifter."

But it doesn't make a difference what I say since they aren't paying one bit of attention to me.

Troy throws his hands up behind his head as he starts to freak out. "Crap. Oh, Crap! Like dude crapola. We're screwed, man. We need to go before he comes out with some buddies."

I smile a little and shake my head while suppressing a laugh. "Troy, relax. He won't do that."

Logan's glare comes back to rest on me. "How do you know that?"

"Because…I know him."

"How well do you know him?"

I look away as I start to blush remembering our night together before I left. "Pretty well."

Logan parts his lips about to say something but just turns away from me. It's Troy who speaks instead.

"Oh, Amberly. Please, tell me you didn't bed that maniac."

Logan's head whips around so fast I swear he could have broken his neck. Feeling like I need to protect him from the breakdown I can see coming in his eyes I almost scream out, "No. It's not like that. We…"

"You what?" Logan says and I can feel the hostility in his voice on my skin.

"We kissed."

"And what else?"

"Nothing…we just kissed."

Logan's eyes go black as he turns away saying, "You should go see how your parents are doing."

"Logan, I –"

"I don't want to talk right now. Go see your parents."

I hesitate for a moment but I really don't want to leave things like this, not with him. "Logan, I didn't tell you about him for many reasons but the main reason is I didn't know how."

"It doesn't matter."

I move a little closer to him. "It matters to me."

Logan turns around to face me and Troy moves further away as he starts to whistle to himself. For once I think *smart boy*.

"We both know there's a reason you didn't tell me about him, tell me I'm wrong."

I look away from Logan for the first time as I say, "I don't know what to say."

"We both know that isn't true."

I have to think for a minute on what he could be talking about and then it hits me. "Logan, I—"

"It doesn't matter."

"No, it does, I just...I don't know what you want me to say."

"Do you love him?"

I look over at Troy, not wanting to look at Logan at the moment. "I don't know. I haven't known him long enough to figure that out."

"Fine," I can see the seriousness in his eyes when he pauses, "Do you love me?"

"Logan."

"What, it's an honest question."

"I...I don't know...we..." Before I even get the chance to fully answer his question Logan's hands are hard on my face and he's pulling me into him. The next thing I know I can feel his warm soft lips on mine. I close my eyes to their touch and move my hands and place them on his dirt-covered shirt right above his heart and I can feel it beating faster with each passing second. A moment later Logan removes his hands from my face and places them on my back just above my butt and applies enough pressure to move me close enough to his chest to where I can feel his body heat melting with mine.

I know he feels it because he pauses for a moment, uncertain, but then my body becomes calm again and he presses his hand on the bare skin of my lower hip. I can feel the calluses on his palm as it rests on my skin but it doesn't bother me. Minutes pass and we are still standing here entertained by both our bodies and our lips. He removes his hand from under my shirt then places it on my cheek once more.

Julian.

My eyes shoot open just before we hear Troy let out a whistle then Logan opens his and pulls away. Not sure of what to say at this point so I just stand there as he looks at me like he too is uncertain. He rubs my cheek before bending down to give me one last peck on the lips and whispers in my ear. "I had to do that at least once...I figured now was a good time."

When we pull away there's a smile on his face but I can see the pain hidden behind it. He starts to walk over toward Troy but not before saying, "Hopefully, that will help you figure things out."

I look over at Troy who is throwing a thumbs up to Logan and then when he looks at me he puts them behind his back and looks away as he starts to whistle again.

I turn away towards the cave but not without looking at Logan once more as he walks over to Troy. And I can see all the pain written on his body. It hurts so much knowing that I'm the one causing it. I start to walk to the cave before I have the chance to change my mind.

I mean how do you choose between someone you've loved your whole life, your first true love, and someone you just met? If only it were that simple. I've waited so many years to hear Logan tell me he loved me back and then when the time comes I meet someone else. Someone who is so very different from everything that Logan represents for me. Logan is my best friend, my home in so many ways and we know everything about each other so it's so easy being with him but Julian. Julian gives me something I fear Logan never can. He understands a part of me I don't understand myself yet and the connection we have runs so much deeper than the one

I've created with Logan over all these years. However, it's more than that with Julian, he makes me feel safe in every sense of the word and just like Logan, he feels like home to me. In only a few short weeks I feel for Julian almost everything I've ever felt for Logan but what does that mean? And how do I choose between two men that I feel so connected to in two very different ways? These thoughts, along with many others, cloud my mind as I make my way away from Logan and closer to Julian as I enter the cave entrance.

Chapter 37

A **aron**

"Where have you been all this time?" I ask her. Not sure of what else to say but you would think that after eighteen long years, I would have some better questions to ask the love of my life.

She touches the blanket hanging in the doorway before saying. "In my village."

"Why didn't you return to the forest?"

"I thought you were dead. I never wanted to enter the forest again after that day. I lost you and my parents and it was too much. The forest became a reminder of everything I lost that night."

I take her in my arms trying to comfort her. "I'm sorry. I should have been there."

"Why didn't you come looking for me?"

"I did. I went into the forest every day trying to pick up on your scent. I did it for nearly nine years. Then I just gave up."

Jocelyn tips her head back far enough to look me in the eyes before saying, "You looked that long?"

I look back into her loving eyes and say, "Yes."

"What did you think happened?"

"I just remember your parents showing up after you passed out in my arms. They were about to take you from me and then the fight broke out. I remember getting stabbed in the stomach by someone I didn't know and then being blasted in the chest with an energy ball." I pause trying to think harder. "As I lay on the ground, moments before I lost consciousness, my eyes found you laying on the ground about fifty feet from me and you were covered in blood. I listened hard for your heart but I heard nothing. Not yours and not our child's."

"It was the same for me. When I woke up I saw you covered in blood and your chest wasn't rising or falling. I was so distraught that I went crazy on everyone around me." She pauses for what feels like forever and digs her hands hard into my back before she says, "After that, I returned to the village and made everyone forget."

Made everyone forget, confused I ask, "What do you mean?"

She moves her head away from my chest and plants her hands there instead as she answers, "I grew stronger over the years. My powers grew. I didn't tell you because I didn't want you to be afraid of me."

I reach down to cup her chin in my hand to make her look up at me as I say in reply, "You could never scare me away. Now tell me... please."

She smiles a smile I haven't seen in years and it makes my heart warm.

"It's hard to explain. I went back to the village and everyone asked where my parents were, what happened, and what was all the noise. So I went into their minds and planted a false memory about what happened to my parents. I know no one knew about you or me being pregnant but they would soon so I had to come up with something."

She pauses for too long so I know she isn't going to continue so I ask, "Then what?"

"I planted a protection spell around the whole village. No one could enter it unless I allowed them or unless they were of our blood."

"And what about your parents?"

Her eyes grow dark and I know I hit a nerve and not a good one.

"What they did was wrong but they were my parents and they didn't deserve to die like that."

"How? What happened?"

I can see her eyes trying to focus on the memory but not really wanting to as she answers, "Men I never saw before came into the forest. When I woke up they were everywhere. I was starting to regain consciousness and I saw my parents were in front of me, I think protecting me from the men we didn't know. First, my mother fell to the ground, and then my father." She closes her eyes before she continues, "These men were strong. They killed everyone except me. And in return, I killed all of them."

"Who?"

Her eyes change back to the loving ones I know and she smiles. "It doesn't matter. All that matters is we are all safe and together again."

She leans back into my chest as I close my eyes. Not realizing how much I missed the curve of her body and the warmth that left her body to enter mine. The feelings I suppressed for all these years are returning in full force and I wonder how I ever lived a day without her. And in this moment I swear to never live another one that way. She is everything to me. Her and my daughter and I will do everything I can to make sure we never leave each other's sides again.

Chapter 38

Amberly

"Is it safe to enter?" I ask to the opening of my father's room.

I can hear a muffled laugh through the crack in the door and it takes me a minute to realize it's my mothers. It's a laugh I've never heard from her before, one that's honest and not reserved. It brings a smile to my face to know that for once she is happy and in many ways it feels like I'm meeting her for the first time.

Even her voice is different as she calls to me from the room, "Yes. Yes, it is."

I push the wooden door and blanket aside to find them huddled together on his bed like it's freezing out and the only way to keep warm is to press up against each other as hard as you can. I have to suppress both a smile and a laugh when I look at them. My mother is almost molded into my father's chest as she lays her head and hands in the same place and his arms are draped around her small body as he looks down at her with a huge smile on his face.

He turns his attention to me but the smile never disappears. "I guess everything is ok outside?"

"Not really," I pause for a moment to look behind me as I think about Logan and Julian rolling around in the dirt throwing punches at each other, over me, only moments before, "but for now I think we can say it is."

My mother pulls away from my father just enough to turn and look at me. "What was that all about anyway?"

For the first time I look away from my parents before I reply, "I really don't want to talk about it."

Aaron's smile leaves his face as he and my mother move further away from each other.

My mother speaks first, "What's going on? I don't know Logan to act like that for no reason." She moves further away from my father and now rests on the edge of the bed, "Troy, that's a different story but Logan he never acts like that unless he feels like he has to."

Still, without looking at her I replied, "It's a long story Mom and one I would much rather talk about at another time." I pause trying to think of something to say to get her to forget about this subject, at least for now. So I try to turn her attention to the only other thing she may turn the conversation towards, "Plus, you two need time. I just wanted to come and see how the reunion was going," I pause for a moment as I gesture at them with my hand in a fleeting motion and then continue, "I see it's going well so I will be leaving now."

I turn to walk out the door but sadly I don't move fast enough. The moment my foot plants itself, readying the other to take its first step for the door, my father is standing in front of me with his hand on the door cutting off my exit. I wish I knew how to move that fast, that's something he really needs to teach me.

"I feel before you leave I should add to what your mother said. I know that Julian can be both rash and arrogant at times but he is not known to just attack someone without probable cause. Especially someone who isn't in the pack." He pauses for a moment to cross his arms over his chest and look at me with that leader gaze of his, praying it will work on me like it does the rest of his pack, "So, please stay awhile and enlighten us."

The smile returns to his face as mine falters knowing that there is no way out of this and that after I tell them what is going on it will be time to face the music and time to figure out who it is I want. And honestly, I'm not at all ready to make that choice.

I let out a sigh and turned away from my father and back to the bed where my mother is still sitting. I look up at him as I say, "You really need to teach me how to do that and soon." At first, he looks at me confused but then it must register to him that I'm talking about how he moves so fast because he smiles at me as he leans against the wall near the door.

My mother's right hand is patting the free spot on the bed to her right asking me to come sit next to her. I slowly lift my feet and make my way over to her unsure of where to start.

Not wanting to be the first to talk, I look around my father's room for the first time. You'd think after all the time I already spent here that I would have seen his room before now but this is the first time. As I look around I realize we are a lot more alike than I ever thought possible. I didn't grow up with him but yet somehow I still got a part of him.

There are books everywhere. Books on the shelves, books on the floor, and a few more next to his bed. Perhaps it's for some light reading before closing his eyes at night. Just like me. I start to wonder if I get that from him or if that is just a mutual hobby.

"Amberly?" My mother's voice pulls me from my thoughts. I turn around so I'm facing her and her expression begs for my explanation.

I sigh and close my eyes, "I don't know where to start."

"Anywhere would be nice," Aaron says from behind me.

Instead of sitting back on the bed, he stays leaning against the far wall with his arms crossed over his chest. Something tells me my mother is the only person he can't get mad at. I've only known him a short time now and I've gotten that look and stance more times than I can count but when he looks at my mother there's nothing but love there.

"Well?" My father's voice pulls me back to the conversation at hand.

"Ok, goodness. Way to rush someone."

Aaron's eyes go wide, and his arms drop to his sides as he straightens himself against the wall. He opens his mouth as if he is about to correct me but then thinks better of it. He slowly closes his mouth again and refolds his arms back over his chest.

I look down at my hands and start to pull my cuticles away from my nails as I think of what to say next. "I've known Logan since I was born and over the years I guess you could say we've gotten closer." At a loss for words, I close my eyes searching for the sentences. "For the longest time, I had feelings for him but not until today was I sure that he reciprocated those feelings," I pause but only for a brief moment, not wanting them to say anything yet I continue, "and in the meantime, while I waited for Logan I started to fall for someone else."

Aaron starts to straighten himself once more as his eyes widen like he knows what I'm about to say and doesn't want me to say it. I turn to look at my mom and smile. "I know today is the first time you got to meet Julian and sadly he wasn't on his best behavior but when I came here he was different. I don't know how to explain it but everyone tells me that since I've been around he's been better. Like I ground him or make him less angry or maybe just bring the best out in him." It's like she knows what I'm talking about as she looks at my father and smiles but his gaze is locked on me as I continue, "He was there for me every step of the way with all this craziness and we got very close because of it."

I can see the wheels turning in my mother's eyes which is why I'm surprised when she asks, "And what does this have to do with what happened outside?"

"Well I guess you could say Julian and I got close, like I said, but closer then Logan and I ever did. I feel something for him that I don't understand and I really can't explain. He makes me feel…different."

"Different?" My mother says as she looks down at her hands.

"Yes." I pause long enough to find the right words and the next thing I know they are pouring out of me so fast that I can't stop them, "I feel like something comes alive in me when I'm with him and I've never been happier. With Logan it's safe and no risk. I don't doubt that he will always be there and always care for me and we know each other like the backs of our hands but…but Julian is different."

I can see my mom trying to make sense of everything I'm saying as she says, "You keep saying that but what does that mean?"

"Like I said I'm not too sure what it means myself. All I know is how I feel when I'm with him and when I'm not with him I want to be."

"Do you love him?" My mom's question lingers in the open space between us.

Aaron drops his arms to his sides again and moves closer for my response.

"I don't know. I don't think so. We haven't known each other long enough for that but I think with time…I could."

I can see my dad's face contort but before he can say anything my mother asks, "And what about Logan? You two grew up together, you've always been inseparable."

"That will never change. I feel, maybe, we missed our shot. Don't get me wrong, I care about Logan more than anything. We have always been there for each other. He means everything to me but…"

"But what?"

I close my eyes not wanting to say it out loud, "He waited too long," I pause for a moment looking for the right words to say next, knowing they never mattered as much as they do right now, "When I met Julian, everything changed."

"So you're telling me if Julian wasn't in the picture you would be with Logan now?"

I look at my mother with sad eyes, "I think so."

My mother stands and I can feel the heat coming from her body. "This is wrong."

"What's wrong?"

I've seen her angry before, hell angry has always been her normal, but this is something else as she puts her hands on her hips and paces the bedroom floor with me and Dad looking at her she says, "This. You and that boy."

Shock takes over as I ask, "What?"

"For starters, you barely know him and you're telling me you are going to give up a boy who has loved you for years, looked out for you, and been there for you, for someone you barely know?"

I can feel the blood running down my cheeks and I know I need to hold my temper in but she is starting to make it impossible. The blood is rushing so quickly that I feel dizzy and the room becomes blurry. "Loved me for years? Mom, wake up because it's the other way around. I've loved him for as long as I can remember and he never once, until today, showed anything other than friendship for me now that I've met someone and it feels right in every cell of my body, you want me to, just walk away from it?" Waiting for her to respond is like waiting for a pig to fly, pointless, "You don't get it."

I can see the disappointment on her face when she says, "You're right, I don't."

"Well, I don't know what to tell you."

I start to stand but I can't feel my feet underneath me. I slowly let myself back down to the bed without them noticing that I even tried to stand.

"Do you still love Logan?" She asks.

I don't answer.

"Well, do you?"

"It's none of your business how I feel. You wanted to know what the fight was about and now you know."

For the first time, my father speaks up. "Actually, we don't. They wouldn't fight just because they both like you. At least I hope they wouldn't."

Now I'm annoyed and I just want the conversation to end so I close my eyes and blurt out, "We kissed OK."

"Who?" My mother asks.

I turn back to her, "Julian and I kissed."

My father's face turns from one of confusion to one that looks annoyed or worried. I'm about to ask him why he looks like that but my mother speaks up first.

"And?"

"And what?"

My mother sighs as she says, "Don't play dumb, it's not your strong suit."

I pull my arms away from my body, wanting to do something with them but not sure what. Knowing there isn't anything, other than punch something I slowly fold my arms over my chest.

"I'm not playing dumb I really don't know what else you want me to say."

"Ok, fine, what about you and Logan?"

I can't help but look at the ground at the sound of his name. The thing is I don't know how to answer her question. Yes we kissed, or I should say he kissed me but then again I didn't stop him. I kissed him back and because of that I'm even more confused now then I was before.

"Amberly." I can hear the question in her voice and I know she knows something more is going on but the question I keep asking myself is what is going on?

I care about them both that much is one hundred percent clear to me. I also know that I do love Logan and I always have but at the same time all I've ever done is sit around and wait for him. Wait for him to see me the way I saw him and now after all this time, after I finally met someone else who broke through my Logan-covered wall, he decides he wants me too. How is that fair? Should I try to make it work with him after all these years? Should I risk our friendship? All over something that might just be a momentary thing for him. I mean he could be confused and even if he isn't it's still taken him all this time to finally address it and now Julian is involved. And with Julian everything is different and I don't wonder or question things with him like I do with Logan. I know deep down I've already made up my mind but still this is probably the hardest decision I'm ever going to have to make and I should probably make sure it's the right choice for everyone involved.

I look up to see both of my parents still looking at me but now my father has his arms braced on the bed like he's trying to hold himself there and his face, well it hasn't changed. My mother however seems more inclined to continue to pace around the bedroom until I answer.

"It's complicated."

My mother lets a small smile creep free. "What relationship isn't?"

"I don't know, you tell me. Because right now I wish they were simpler."

Her smile disappears. "Honey, talk to us, maybe we can help."

I close my eyes as I mumble. "I doubt it."

"You never know."

As I sigh, in the same breath I say, "Logan and I kissed too."

I hear a sigh come from the direction of the bed where my father still stands but I can't make myself look at him. Only knowing him for a short time doesn't seem to register in my brain. Ever since I found out he was my father it's like he has been there all along. Like I was never without one and I'm still looking for his approval, as any child would and in a way, it really annoys the hell out of me.

I can finally feel my feet again and the lightheadedness is gone so I stand up slowly and make my way over to the door, with my back to my parents.

When did my life get so confusing and crazy? Oh, yeah I forgot, maybe it was the moment I talked to a wolf or the moment I found out my dad was still alive or the moment Logan finally kissed me, or how about when I found out I was part wolf. Nope, I think it all went to hell when I met Julian. That was the moment everything shifted, that was the moment I came undone.

My mother places her hand on my shoulder and starts to slowly turn me around to face her but I just continue to look at the ground not sure what I'll see in her eyes and knowing I can't take much more right now. I know she wants to keep talking about this but I just don't have it in me right now. Without another word, I turn away and head to the door but with each step my legs get heavier and heavier and the dizziness starts to return. Not able to take another step, I stop in my tracks.

"Honey, are you OK?" My mother's words are the last thing I hear before I feel my body sink to the floor.

Chapter 39

Logan

"Dude, I can't believe you finally grew the balls to kiss her," Troy says as he slaps me on the back.

I close my eyes trying to ignore him but that's not so easy when Troy is being Troy. He's way too loud to ignore and way too eager to be heard. Hell, he's waited for this for years. By that I mean he knew how I felt about Amberly long before I did and he kept telling me one day I would realize it and that he wanted to be there the day it happened. The thing is, I knew about a year ago that I loved her but I never wanted to change our friendship so I always hid my feelings far enough away from her, until today that is.

I don't know what made me do it. Maybe it was because I just couldn't hide it anymore, or maybe, it was because I could feel her slipping away from me but right now I can't tell the difference. The only thing I can think about is how she kissed me back.

"Man, what's wrong? You've been waiting to do that for a while and now that you have I thought you'd be a little more... I don't know perky."

I turn to face him when I say, "Perky? That's the word you're going to use right now?"

Troy lifts his hand to his chin and looks to the sky. It's his thinking pose. "Alright, then how about lively or no, no wait I got it," Troy's eyes go wide as he throws his arms in the air, one on either side of his body, and his palms facing out to the sky, "How about spry?"

I look at him with bewilderment. "What did you just say?"

Troy's smile disappears as his arms come back down to lie at his sides. "I said how about the word spry?"

"I can't believe you even know what that word means."

Troy's face contorts with annoyance and he looks at me, both hands on his hips and a look that could kill, and yet I can't seem to help needing to stifle a laugh.

"I'll have you know I know many big words. Maybe even some you don't."

"Oh, I'm sure about that."

His arms lower to his sides once more as I turn away from him and make my way towards the cave. I can hear the leaves moving under his feet as he follows me with haste.

"No, really I do."

Chapter 40

Angela

Since Amberly and her mother arrived everything has been in an uproar around the cave. The pack can't stop talking about how everything is about to change. Change is normally a good thing but right now it has me a little unsettled. Aaron and this pack are all I've ever really known and I don't know what I would do if he left. This is something he's always prayed for and it would be wrong of me to take that or wish it away but a part of me is hoping he doesn't leave and I would be lying if I said I wasn't.

My thoughts are interrupted when my gaze runs across Julian. He's sitting in the dark far away from everyone with his head in his hands. I thought he would be happy that she was back but he seems the opposite. I make my way over to his side but when I get close enough he looks at me and gets up and walks away. I watch him as he exits the cave and I follow behind.

"Julian." He keeps walking so this time I yell at the top of my lungs, "Julian, stop."

With much hesitation, he stops dead but doesn't turn around when he says, "What do you want, Angela?"

"What's going on with you?"

I'm a few feet away from him but I can still hear him sigh before he says, "Nothing. I just want to be left alone."

"But Amberly's back, don't you want to go talk to her?"

"No."

Confusion is starting to take over as I reach his side, "Julian, you're making no sense what's going on?"

"It doesn't matter."

"It matters to me," I say as I place my hand on his shoulder.

"I need your help with something and you're not going to want to do it."

I take my hand away and place it at my side before I reply, "Julian, you should know me better than that. I'm always here, whatever you need. But you need to tell me what's going on."

Julian turns to face me and that's when I see the hurt, it's clear all over his body that he's breaking in a way I've never seen before. Then my eyes come to rest on his wet face and that's when I realize he's been crying. Julian, crying.

I reach out and take his hand but he won't look me in the eyes even when I say, "What do you need?"

Some time passes and then he finally looks at me as he says, "I need you to help make her hate me."

Confusion is plain on my face when I say, "Who? Amberly?"

Looking away now he answers, "Yes."

"Why? I don't understand."

Julian turns his back towards me again as he takes his hand out of mine, "It doesn't matter why, all that matters is it needs to be done."

"Julian, you love her so why do you want her to hate you?"

"Because it's for the best. So are you going to help me or do I need to find someone else?"

I close my eyes and let out a sigh before I reply, "I'll help you but first, you need to tell me why."

"Because I'm no good for her and unless I make her hate me we will never walk away from each other."

I can feel all his hurt radiating off of him and it's making me want to cry myself. I've known Julian for many years and never have I seen him cry and nothing has ever bothered him or broken him, not till now. I'm searching for the right words to say but I have none so he takes the silence as a need to keep talking.

"I thought the fight would be enough but it wasn't. That much became obvious after I heard her talking to her parents."

I don't think I've ever been this confused before, "Wait what fight and what talk?"

I can hear the smile in his next words, "Well I kind of punched her human, more than once or twice."

I can't help but place my face in my hands on that one. I shake my head back and forth not sure what to say to him but that doesn't matter because he continues.

"And then I went to talk to her father but she was already in there with him and," the smile is all gone from his voice now, only the pain is clear when he continues, "that's when it became clear to me that I need to do something."

"Julian, you're still not making much sense."

He turns around before replying, "She loves Logan. That human."

I try to hide my surprise before I say, "You heard her say this?"

"In so many words yes but I could also hear her mother's approval of him and her dislike of me."

Trying to make light of the mood I let out a little scoff as I said, "Since when do you take Amberly as the listening to authority type?"

"It's not just that. It's wrong we shouldn't be together, Aaron doesn't want it and," he pauses for what feels like an eternity and when he continues I can hear all the hurt in his words as his voice breaks, "I'm not good enough for her. I know it, you know it, everyone knows it. So that's where you come in."

"Meaning?"

I can see how lost he is in his eyes before he looks away and taking me by surprise he says, "I need you to kiss me."

* * *

Amberly

Ever since the truth came out and I met Julian, I seem to be having a hard time staying conscious and I'm beginning to wonder what's wrong with me. When I open my eyes again my parents are standing over me. Before I can form a word I feel the necklace around my neck get hotter and hotter till I reach up without a second thought and rip it from my neck. I look at it dangling in my hand swaying side to side in front of my face and it's the only thing I can see. Before I opened my eyes I could hear my parents saying my name in anxious tones and even as they continued to say my name their voices sounded further away from me with each passing moment.

My eyes and attention want to go to my parents but the amulet is all I can focus on, it's drawing me in. Moments pass and my surroundings change, everything's so blurry that I can't make out where I am. I can feel the dirt and leaves under my bare feet so I know I'm in the woods but where and how did I get here? I hear yelling up ahead so I start to stumble through the woods using the trees and smells to guide me. Hoping that someone can tell me what's going on. Then suddenly without any warning, everything gets really bright and something really hot hits me and I end up on my ass. When

178

I pull my hands away from my chest they are covered in blood and I can see clearly. Up ahead there are men in all black throwing these white and black balls out of their hands. Two of them notice me as one starts to walk over.

"You? How are you here? You're not even born yet!"

Bewildered, all I can say is, "Wh...what?"

The man smiles down at me, "My thoughts exactly."

I try to get up and make a run for it but before the thought makes its way to my body the man steps on my leg hard and I scream in agony. When I can move again I look up to see he's almost a foot taller than the other man, who is now starting to make his way over to us, and he has a deep scar that runs the length of the left side of his face from eyebrow to lip and he has chocolate brown messy hair that looks like it hasn't been washed in weeks. The other man reaches us finally and I notice he must be around 5'8" in height and he's a little heavier with long raven hair to his shoulders.

As I'm trying to figure out who these men are I hear the one with the raven-colored hair say, "Lurch, shouldn't we tell Vladimir about this?"

"Let me think Onyx," as the man Lurch puts his fingers to his chin, like he's thinking, I can tell he's annoyed but I don't understand why, "Why would we tell him when it would only make him mad?"

Confused, the one named Onyx says, "But why?" Then the realization becomes clear on his face as I can almost see the wheels turning in his head, "Oh, yea. That would mean we failed at our task." Then his gaze comes to rest on me, still on the ground. "So what do we do now? I mean we could kill her here but then she will still be alive now."

Seeing that I'm not the only one confused when I look at the one named Lurch, I think maybe I'll get some kind of answer as he opens his mouth but then looks at me and closes it again. He gestures to his comrade to follow him before he slams his foot back down hard on my leg till I hear it snap and scream in pain once more. With a smile on his face, he walks about ten feet away with Onyx and I can see they are talking but I can't hear anything. Annoyed, I think about how I have wolf DNA in me, and maybe if I focus enough I could hear them.

I close my eyes and take in a slow deep breath and try to dig deep down inside where that part of me is hidden. I feel something shift just a little as the hairs on my arm stand up straight and a warm feeling works its way through my body. I open my eyes wide and that's when I hear them.

"Lurch, I think we should just kill them all now before any more escape."

I can hear the annoyance in his voice when he replies, "You know we can't do that. He wanted them back alive and he has a longer and larger plan in the works, so if we kill them that won't work."

"I know but whatever we do here today obviously isn't enough because she's still alive and doesn't seem changed. She must be at least eighteen so who's to say at that time she didn't mess everything up?"

"That's a great question but the better one is how did she get here?"

Onyx looks back at me before saying, "Well she is from both villages is she not?"

I can see the wheels turning before Lurch says, "I still don't think that would give her this kind of power. I mean yes she is born of both villages so there is a lot we won't know about what she can do but she seems just as surprised," he pauses long enough to look in my direction before continuing, "which leads me to believe that she doesn't know what is about to happen here or what the plan is either."

Then Onyx turns to look at me with a little confusion on his face, "Are you sure she can't hear us?"

"She doesn't seem to know anything about how strong she is or else she would have healed her leg by now so I doubt she knows how to harness her powers yet."

"So what do we do now then? Before she figures everything out I mean."

I can see a devilish look in Lurch's eyes when he looks at me as he says, "We get some answers and have a little bit of fun while we do so."

Then they both look at me and smile as they make their way back over to where I'm laying on the ground.

* * *

Amberly

"Stop." I scream, "Why are you doing this?"

"Because we need some answers, plus it's fun," says the man with the scar running down his face.

The knife feels hot against my skin as he trails it down my chest. The pain is overwhelming, and I can barely think. I can feel blood dripping down my skin, in many different places, all over my body. The only thing I can think of right now is that if I don't stop it I will bleed out in a matter of hours, if not sooner.

The men named Lurch and Onyx have been asking me questions for what feels like hours now. Things like where I live, who my parents are, what my powers are, my age and how I got here. They also asked me the year. The thing they don't realize is by asking their own questions they have answered some of my own. I now have no doubt in my mind that I'm in the past. I'm pretty sure this is the same night that my parents were talking about, the same night my grandparents were murdered. But what I can't figure out is how I got back here or how to get back home. I also don't understand why they are here?

As if on cue to answer another one of my questions Onyx turns to Lurch and asks in a hushed tone, just not hushed enough for me not to hear, "The boss wants her but her mother got away so should we go after her? Maybe that will take care of the whole problem."

Lurch looks at him with annoyance all over his face, "The boss wanted this done without everyone knowing about us and if we go after her we will have to wipe out the whole village and that's not part of the plan. At least not yet anyway."

Now more than ever I know I need to get back so I close my eyes and concentrate as hard as I can. I got myself here so I know there has to be a way to get myself back. I try everything I can but nothing works. Annoyed, I lay back on the ground and look at the blue and red sky and the only thing that popped in my head was Julian. The thought of never seeing him again is starting to weigh me down in a way I didn't know was possible. I thought if

181

anyone would make me feel like this it would be either my parents or Logan but when I think about them the pull isn't as strong.

And that's when it hits me, I sit up fast and close my eyes once more and focus on his face, his touch, his voice, anything that I can think of and without realizing it I say his name. I open my eyes to see Lurch and Onyx running towards me screaming as I feel myself being pulled at from behind. I close my eyes again and focus on seeing him again and feeling his arms around me.

"Julian."

In seconds a cold that I've never felt before engulfs me and I hear familiar voices.

Chapter 41

Aaron

I take one last look at Amberly on the bed as if she's sleeping. That amulet, I knew it was going to be a problem and now all I can do is hope and pray she will wake up. Not even her mother knows what's going on. One minute she's talking, more like arguing, with us and the next her legs give out. She rips off the amulet and stares into it like there's never been anything so pretty and then she passes out. Everything about that amulet and everything about this situation feels wrong. Julian comes into focus and before I can stop myself I make my way over to him and grab him by the arm and haul him outside into the forest.

"What's going on?" He asks in a confused tone.

Not sure how to start the conversation so I just come right out with it, "Amberly, she fainted again, Angela is looking her over," his eyes wander back to the cave and I know this conversation is going to be a lot harder, "did you kiss my daughter?" I stop and let his arm go and he turns to face me.

I can sense his hesitation as he looks at me, "Yes."

I can't help but grind my teeth as I ask, "Why?"

"You're asking like I did it because I had to or like I knew I wasn't supposed to so I did it anyway like a disobedient ass."

"Well how am I supposed to know why you did it? You don't have the best track record with women, Julian, or for authority either if we are being honest here."

Julian looks away from me as he digs his shoe into the ground, "I love her that's why I did it."

I let out a sigh, this was the answer I was afraid of.

"I know I'm not supposed to and that I can't and I'm not good enough but I don't have a choice. It's not like I want to love her I just do and I can't help or change it. Believe me I've tried."

I close my eyes and run my hand over my face, "And what do you want me to do about this information?"

"I don't know. I don't think there is anything either of us can do. And it doesn't matter anyway she has that dude Smolden or whatever his name is."

I try to fight off a laugh but it comes out low anyway. "His name is Logan and why would you say that?"

Julian turns around to look at the trees, "I saw them kiss. After you retired to the cave he kissed her and she let him. And it wasn't an ordinary kiss, it was one full of passion and longing. I could smell it on, not only him but her too."

Julian cut off abruptly and I knew there was more to it than that. "And?"

He turns to look at me trying to hide it but he knows I know and looks back at the ground. "I can hear her thoughts better than anyone else's and after some time passed, she said my name and opened her eyes to pull away from the kiss but Logan ended it first."

"Julian, I-"

Julian holds up his hand and looks to the cave entrance, "You don't need to worry about me, I'm backing off. I know I can't be with her, it's not allowed. So all I ask for is when the time comes that you let me be the one to protect and look after her. I know you'll agree that no one could do it better than me because I love her so I would die to protect her and other than that I need your help with one other thing."

I look at him, not sure of what to say. "And what would that be?"

Julian closes his eyes. "I need you to help me make her hate me."

* * *

Logan

"You're a piece of work, you know that?"

Troy tries to stuff the bread in his mouth faster as he looks around to make sure no one sees him eating it. I can't help but laugh at him as we turn the corner and I see everyone huddled up and whispering. I look around the room and see Jocelyn sitting down and someone rubbing her back, I don't know who. I see tears in her eyes even from this distance and I know something's wrong. My heart skips a beat as I make my way through the crowd to her side. Troy notices and quickly falls in step behind me.

"Jocelyn?" She looks up to meet my eyes with hers. "What's going on?"

"It's Amberly. She fainted and she's running a high fever and they don't know what's wrong with her."

I feel my knees buckle and if it wasn't for Troy behind me and his strong arms on my back I think I would have fallen to the ground. "Where is she?"

She pointed to her room and without another word I made my way through the crowd once more to the room she was in. I make it through the threshold and then there are arms on me holding me back.

"Let me go." When the hands don't remove themselves from my body I say it again almost with a growl. "I said let me go."

I see Julian come around the corner and to my surprise he puts a hand on the one guy's shoulder and says, "Let him pass."

I don't waste another moment on him as I make my way into the room. I see Aaron as he nods his head in my direction and begins to gather everyone up and take them out of the room until it's just me and Amberly left. Julian is the last one out and our eyes connect as he closes the door behind him and I can not only see but also feel the pain that lingers there.

I turn to Amberly as she lies on the bed like she's asleep and I take her hand in mine and it's freezing which makes no sense since she's running a fever. I lift my free hand to place it on her head and smooth out her hair so I can lean in to kiss her on the forehead.

"You're going to be OK, Amberly." I whisper and I feel her hand grip mine.

I lift my head away from hers to look her over and when I notice there's no change I look away and sigh. "What's going on with you? You don't talk to me anymore."

She squeezes my hand again and I can't help but smile but when I look at her, her face is contorted with pain and I know something's wrong. I look her over and I see the fabric of her shirt just below her heart is red. I lightly lift the hem of the shirt up and I see a deep gash.

"That wasn't there a second ago." I turn to give her hand a kiss and make my way out the door to get someone but then I feel something wet and sticky on my hand and I turn over her arm to see a long cut running down the length of it.

"Aaron, Julian!" I scream for anyone who can hear me and I can't believe I called for him of all people but I don't know what else to do. I hear footsteps running around outside the door and when I turn back to look at her, her legs begin to kick slightly as I look down at them to see another stain take form on her clothes. I lift her clothes away from her leg to see a deep gash trailing upwards as I watch.

"Aaron!" I scream louder this time.

I put her clothes back in place on her leg and grab her hand again and kiss her knuckles as I hear her whisper, "Julian," as the door opens behind me and Julian and Aaron walk into the room. I can tell by the look on Julian's face that he heard her say his name.

Aaron moves past him to stand next to me. "What's wrong?"

I look up at him and turn her arm over to show him the long cut. "She's bleeding."

Aaron steps back. "What-"

Then the woman Angela enters the room and once her eyes come to rest on Amberly she says. "We need to give her blood, she is losing too much too fast and if I don't do something soon she will die."

"Great, that's one solution but what do we do to stop whatever this is?" Julian says.

Angela looks at him with sad eyes like she knows something the rest of us in the room don't. "I don't know yet. It looks like something I encountered many years ago but I need time to look her over to see if I'm right. But first we need to stop the bleeding and set her up with someone to give her blood."

"I'll do it," I say as I start to strip off my shirt.

Angela looks at me, and I mean really looks at me and smiles. I begin to feel a little uncomfortable but it doesn't matter. I sit on the other side of Amberly and take her hand as Angela comes over and ties something around the upper part of my arm and I feel a little sting as I watch her connect a tube to one end and then she sticks it into Amberly's arm. I watch the blood run down my end into hers and I smile as I think to myself now we are truly connected.

"What now?" I hear Julian say to Angela.

"I have to stitch up the wounds or the blood he's giving her won't make a difference."

Julian isn't paying any attention as we all look at him and his face gets whiter as he walks over to where I'm sitting. We all follow his eyes as another deep gash makes its way down her chest. He looks at Angela, "We don't have much time."

Chapter 42

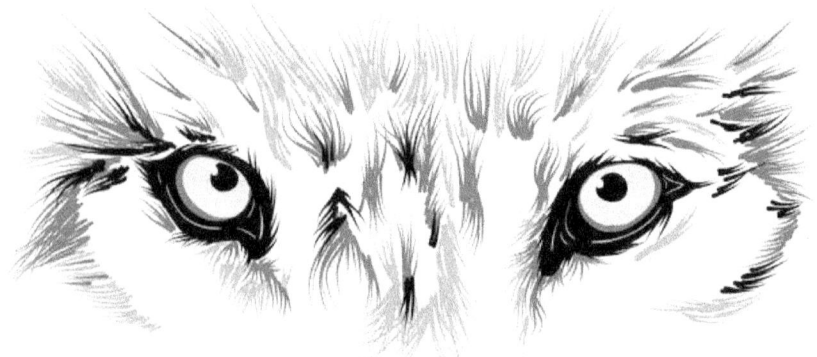

Amberly

I open my eyes slowly, they feel like they are glued shut for a moment until shapes start to become visible. I see Angela standing over me first then I look at the person holding my hand, it's Logan. My eyes wander around the room until I see him, Julian. I want to tell him everything right now, how I feel and how he is the one thought that brought me back but then I hear the door open and Aaron and my mom walk up behind him and a smile of relief starts to form on their faces and I hate so much that I'm about to take that away from them.

So many conversations need to be had right now but the most important words are the next ones that come out of my mouth.

"Their coming."

A bunch of confused faces look at me until my father breaks the silence, "Who's coming?"

I look at my mother then, knowing she is the only one who will be able to make any sense out of my words, "The men from that night. The night you thought you lost everything. They are coming and they won't stop till they get what they want this time."

Julian's voice feels so far away when it reaches me, "And what do they want?"

I turn to look at him with sorrow-filled eyes as I say, "Me."

Thank You For Reading

You can make a difference

Reviews go a long way and help all authors but for us indie/self-published authors it's the most important as it helps our work get more notice. We self-published authors don't have the marketing others get with a publisher. However, I feel I have something better than they do. I have committed and loyal readers that I appreciate more than anything. Without you reading and reviewing, my dream would be only that, but now it's becoming a reality. So thank you. Honest reviews of my books help bring them to the attention of other readers. So, if you enjoyed this book please take a moment and head over to Amazon and Goodreads and leave your honest review because they help more than you know.

About the Author

Laura Lukasavage started writing shortly after her mother's passing when she was only fourteen years old. She remembered how her mom would write poems and letters to her stepdad and as a way to feel close to her mother she took up writing. She started with poems in eighth grade and short stories in high school. Once she started college in 2009 at Neumann University in Aston, PA her interest only grew. By the time she would transfer from Neumann to Rowan University in Glassboro, NJ in 2011, after her father's passing, is when she knew what her passions truly were. She majored in Radio, TV and Film productions with a minor in creative writing. She found her love of film and writing meshed together and this is where she felt at peace. Laura writes as a way to escape from reality but to also deal with life as a whole. She writes hoping that one day her books will be an escape for someone needing them just like the books she read in high school to escape the recent loss of her mother.

https://publishingdreams20.wixsite.com/my-site

http://www.insmtagram.com/lauralukasavageauthor

http://www.tiktok.com/@angelsguideme23?lang=en

Also by Laura Lukasavage

Author of Fantasy and Women's Fiction. Series and standalone.

THE DARK INHERITANCE SERIES

BOOK TWO

Moonlight Changes

Laura Lukasavage

Moonlight Changes (Book 2)

Amberly's life is anything but normal. Finding out the truth behind who she really was didn't even crack the surface of all the changes coming her way. Learning she is being hunted by someone hundreds of years old is the least of her problems. Dreamwalking into another shape-shifter mind that needs her help only adds to her troubled life. But when she starts having visions and seeing everyone, she loves dead at her feet she starts to scrabble against the clock. Wanting only to train, and become stronger, so that she can protect the ones she loves from their horrible fate. But can fate be stopped? However, the new shapeshifter isn't the only person she's dreamwalking with. She finds Vladimir's right hand, Aidan invading her mind more than once. Who is he? Why does he feel so familiar to her? While dealing with all the changes in her powers and turning eighteen, she's trying to find some stability in her life and her love life is anything but that. But catching Julian kissing the new girl is only the start of her world unraveling at the seams. How is she supposed to learn how to control her powers, learn to shift and defend herself when her heart is broken? Knowing Vladimir is coming for her and the ones she loves, she wipes away the tears and goes to work. She will do anything to make sure her vision doesn't come to pass.

Moonlight Legacy

THE DARK INHERITANCE SERIES

BOOK THREE

Moonlight Legacy

Laura

Serenity:

It's all happening as I've seen in my dreams. Amberly learned who she was. Was united with those she should have known her entire life. Met her true mate. And then was torn from us all. But hope still springs, because in being lost, Amberly will find answers and learn the true strength of her heart. The last battle might have been lost, but the war has only just begun. And Amberly's choices from here on will send out ripples that will shape the future of our world. But can an eighteen-year-old choose the right path when darkness and grief obscures every way forward?

Enough Is Enough

My name is Elena and I have put a plan in motion to escape my abuser and recurring nightmare. However, there is that old saying about the best-laid plans going awry... Escaping your abuser only to have new obstacles laid out in front of you. Now not only does my body need to heal but my mind as well. Beaten, torn down, and broken. I'm no longer the woman I once was and to find her again will be no easy task. Anxiety takes over my mind and body whenever any man gets too close. Even if it was someone I knew would never hurt me. Can I overcome this fear? Can I get close to a man again and live out the rest of my life in peace, or am I destined to be alone and afraid for the rest of my days? A story of a broken woman fighting to stabilize her life after ending her abuse. Can she silence the fears in her mind and allow herself a happy ending with her lifelong friend Jason, or will the anxiety and fear her husband beat into her win out? Jim has become Elena's living nightmare but today everything changes. Elena has put her plan in motion. A plan to take back both her life and happiness a

See You On The Other Side

...death isn't goodbye

See You On The Other Side

Laura Lukasavage

Blissfully happy, newlyweds Sam and Jane are looking forward to years of building their life together. But the reality they thought would be theirs is shattered by tragedy when Jane dies. Now both Sam and Jane are lost in the darkness alone. Unable to see any way forward. Only by finding her way to peace can Jane help pull Sam out of the depths of his grief. But can he be saved when the love of his life has been ripped away from him, taking the future they planned together with her?

Will's Awakening (Book 1 In the Dark Awakening Series)

Will Walker's life is about to change forever as destiny finds us all one way or another.

His life shattered to pieces the day his older brother West was murdered, and their father disappeared from his life overnight. His mother is the only person left in his life until his childhood best friends, Thea and Trey, fight to make amends.

Will is facing demons of his own that he fears he can't outrun and that may keep him from the normal life that he craves so badly.

He's being hunted in his dreams by the Company and their leader Morpheus and soon realizes that there was more to his brother's death than anyone knew, but Will holds a more profound secret.

Will soon discover he may be the only hope the world has against Morpheus. Will he be the world's savior or their doom?

www.ingramcontent.com/pod-product-compliance
Lightning Source LLC
Chambersburg PA
CBHW051510260626
47162CB00008B/2899